The LESSON

RANDY GETROST

ISBN 978-1-0980-0039-4 (paperback)
ISBN 978-1-0980-0040-0 (digital)

Christian Faith Publishing, Inc.
832 Park Avenue
Meadville, PA 16335
www.christianfaithpublishing.com

Printed in the United States of America

This book is in memory of my father Jerry Getrost, the finest man I have ever known.

Lesson: An activity that you do in order to learn something, also something that is taught. A single class or part of a course of instruction. Something learned from experience.

PROLOGUE

Here I sit on the front porch of this old house, pondering the events of the three days just passed. I can smell the scent that can only come from a place like this. It is a product of this environment, a plethora of, or perhaps an accumulation of events that have been completed or are in process. Not unpleasant, all. In fact, comforting and uncomfortable at the same time.

As a child, I sat on this porch often. The memories that surround me seem to have taken on a life of their own. They not only exist in the past but seem very real in the now. At this moment, they are almost palpable. It is funny how the mind connects smells with memories. For instance, when I smell lilac, I see my grandma. When I smell old spice cologne, I see my grandpa. In the same way at this moment, my olfactory system is activating memories I had pushed deep in my mind.

I smile a sad smile. No one sees. I brush a tear away. No one sees. I say, "I'm sorry." No one hears.

The old paths here are grown over, but you can still see where our young feet once traveled. The lesson started a long time ago. My grandfather told me this: "All learning starts with not knowing."

As I look at the old paths and think on the path that brought me back to this place. I turn my attention forward. Why is the next step hidden? Where am I to go? I wish you were here. Am I lost or just not yet found?

I miss you. Yes, I know you trained me for this. At this moment, I could use your advice. Ah, there you are. In my mind's eye, I see you—calm. You tell me, "Speak to the storm." A quiet spirit, a still mind, all storms must pass.

I settle back into the porch swing and note the breeze has shifted. I settle back into my memory and note the lesson is not over.

Even though you have been gone for a long time, I don't go anywhere without you. You are fixed in my heart, soul, and spirit. It seems that the best way to proceed is to chronicle the events leading up to this moment. So let's walk through them together.

CHAPTER 1

The Homecoming

When I arrived at the old plantation, I was disturbed that it was in such disarray. It is disconcerting when real life does not match up with expectation. Yes, I know, expectations are preplanned disappointments.

For a while, I just sat in my truck, observing the lack of activity. This place had once been alive with the activities of my family but now resembled a picture that had hung on the wall of an abandoned house—a picture I had looked at before but one that would cause memories to spring to the forefront of my mind as I examined it. The picture itself was not the memory but a part of a larger tapestry, one woven over the years. The thing about a tapestry is you must step back from it to see the whole thing. Looking at it up closely, you see only the frames of the finished product. I am brought to the realization that even my memories of this place are frames of a bigger event. I know why I came. I don't know why I am here.

As I step out of my truck, the air seems to be heavy, it almost has weight. I consider the thought that it is not barometric pressure that I discern but something else—a burden, perhaps a spiritual malady. I say out loud to no one in particular, "I am home," and no one cares.

As I start to walk the grounds, it is as though I had let go of it, but it had never let go of me. Evidently my initial impression was incorrect, or the property sensed my presence. It seemed that suddenly it was alive with activity. There was the rattle and chatter of squirrels in the trees, the chirping of birds, insects buzzing. A frog croaking in the pond and a thumping that I could not at first distinguish where it came from. I stopped and listened carefully. It was a heart—my heart.

I took some deep breaths to settle my pulse and remembered your words. "Calm mind." *There we go, okay, now let's regroup*, I tell myself. Regrouping is achieved. Where do I start? The property beckons though somewhat ominously. One step at a time seems appropriate. Here I go.

The house lays straight ahead, and the old cobblestone walk seems to be in good enough shape to traverse.

Yes, I have already forgotten my profound plan. I have not taken one step yet. I am just standing there, looking at the house. Ah yes, the house.

One of the laws of thermodynamics is that nature left to itself will always go to its lowest form of energy and its highest form of disorder. This place does not feel like that, and if it was, it has changed quickly. In the Bible, we find references to objects of nature remembering, and nature itself is said to be yearning. I don't know about nature, but I am both remembering and yearning.

Emerson and Thoreau were called American prophets of eco-wisdom. I, on the other hand, am just a man standing in front of his past, uncomfortable and rambling about notions and theories to keep from going into an old house.

I think I have already said this once, "Here I go," and there I went—down the cobblestone into the jaws of my past. I am having a problem discerning between anticipation and apprehension. I remember quite clearly what my dad told me about bullies, and as I prepare to face my demons, I remember what happened when I stood up to the two bullies in my life. One backed down and the other one cleaned my clock.

I, of course, am a much more mature man now. Obviously, I am not afraid, I am just being cautious, I tell myself. There is nothing here but memories. The people are, however, on their way.

As I follow the cobblestone sidewalk toward the door of "the house," the ominous feeling fades and is replaced by one of expectation, maybe more like presumption. Something is coming; I will not be alone for long. I am not afraid. I am hopeful. The events in my life that occurred in this house had much to do with forming the man that I am.

I suddenly seem very aware of time, and I glance at my watch. I have been on property for two hours already and have not made it inside the house.

"The man that I am," I ask myself, "what does that mean?"

There is a teaching, albeit a psychological device, to help us understand ourselves. It is called the Johari window. If you will, imagine in your mind's eye a window with four separate panes—the first pane being what you know about yourself and everyone else knows, the second pane being what you know about yourself and no one else knows, the third pane being what others see and you don't, the fourth pane being what you don't see in yourself and no one else does either. The reality is that I am not sure I want to look in the fourth pane. The truth is I'm not that happy about the other three. It is my assumption that during this walk down memory lane that there may be some broken window panes.

Here I am, at the front door. It may not sound ominous to you, but it sure feels that way to me. I look under the old flower pot, and the key is right where Joseph said it would be. I pick it up and wipe it off and inspect it closely. I realize the significance of the term *key*. One definition is "something of significant or paramount importance." Another is "to allow or prevent entrance." It would seem I have arrived at a key moment in this journey. The irony is not lost on me as I prepare to use the key to allow my "entrance" into a place my fear has "prevented" me from going for many years now. There is no doubt that this is a significant moment. The tapestry maker is fast at work. The wheel is spinning.

Calm mind, I tell myself. *Calm mind.*

I put the key in the keyhole, and as I steel myself to turn it, I hear a noise behind me. I quickly turn and catch a glimpse of movement in the shadows surrounding the barn. Where did he or she come from? I have been here for quite a while, and I have not seen or heard anything that would have indicated I was not the only one here. I leave the key in the lock, and I head for the barn. Whoever it was must know I am here.

As I approach the barn, it casts a shadow across the yard and over my soul. I turn back and look at the house, sensing movement behind me. The key is gone.

What is going on here? Now I am starting to get mad. I holler at the top of my lungs, "What do you want?" So much for a calm mind.

As I enter the barn, I can sense that there is no one in here. I choose to explore its contents later. For now, I am looking for my tormentor, and they will not like me when I find them.

I turn quickly and trace my steps back to the front door. I grab the handle to shake the door and surprise—it opens into the house. I do not know if it was unlocked beforehand or if my tormentor unlocked it with the key they took. I step into the house, all my senses on full alert.

The foyer is dusty but unchanged. The old coat rack shaped like a bush from an Alfred Hitchcock movie sits in the corner. Man, I hate to see that thing almost as much as I do clowns. My cousin used to tell me that if it did not like you, it would not let you get your coat back. So I never hung my coat on it. Never in my life did I hear of it keeping someone's coat, so either it liked everyone, or it was a lie. I think it liked everyone except me, so I never put my coat on it. I think it knows. Okay, let's keep this moving. This is no time for reminiscing. I almost forgot to stay mad.

Ready or not, here I come!

CHAPTER 2

The Hunt

After my initial encounter with the dangerous coat rack, I move through the foyer slowly and enter the great room. The furniture is politely covered with drop cloths, as though that will keep the memories at bay. In my mind's eye, I look at the room and visualize the pieces of furniture that are hidden under the cloths. The old armchair that Grandma sewed and did her needlepoint work in. It was also the chair that the actual running of the property was directed from. Next to it sets Grandpa's chair. This was the seat that the spoken commands that ran the property came from, but we all knew who the commander really was.

Grandma and Grandpa had a great system, and it worked for them. It was a time when men did not take orders from a woman very well. However, the genuine business mind of the two was Grandma. Grandma and Grandpa were partners in every sense of the word. They both knew their strengths and their weaknesses. And they protected each other. No, they complimented each other, though seldom with words, I might add. Their love for one another was complicated but also deep, and they did not need anyone else to hear them say it. But I digress, which seems to be a common theme in this dissertation.

As I approach the beautiful fireplace that Grandpa built with stones that he and Grandma collected from all over the property, my mind goes back to the many nights I spent sitting in front of it. The spot above it where once hung a portrait of my grandparents now is just an old hook it used to hang on. The portrait was painted many years ago by a local artist that achieved some fame for his work, but my guess is that painting held significance to only my family. The artist's name was Brady Mason. He was commissioned by the United States Army to paint battle scenes during World War II. He never came home. To this day, he is officially listed as missing in action.

All around the room now, I take notice of the spots where objects used to be. All around the room, I take notice of the spots where I used to be. It appears I am close to being in the wrong place and far from being in the right place. I want to leave but staying seems to be the right thing to do. The hunt must continue.

I pass the fireplace and move slowly into the dining room. It seems that there are shadows everywhere in this room. Memories flit across my mind as I survey the room looking for signs of the intruder. I seem to be alone in here with my memories, and I see no sign that anyone else has been here before me. I don't like being toyed with, and I am steadily becoming more annoyed by this chain of events.

Calm mind, I remind myself.

The heck with a calm mind! I run through the dining room into the kitchen with abandon, thinking I will catch this someone off-guard. I am wrong. All I catch is my foot on the door frame, and down I go. I sprawl onto the dusty kitchen floor and let out a yelp as I bang my chin on the floor. I taste my own blood in my mouth and realize I have bitten my tongue badly.

Furious now at the suspected intruder and embarrassed that they might have seen my misadventure, I jump to my feet and spit out a mouthful of blood. I glance around quickly and see no sign of an audience to my fall.

I tell myself, "Take a breath and calm yourself, man." This is getting out of hand. The kitchen is empty, and as much as I dislike clowns, I feel like one at this moment.

CHAPTER 3

The Lion's Den

I must decide whether to go into the mud room off the kitchen, which would take me out to the backyard or turn around and go back into the dining room. I opt for the dining room and decide to head to Grandpa's old den.

"The Lion's Den" was what we called it when we were kids. There were two reasons why we called it that—the first one and the primary one was that Grandpa had a cougar pelt on the wall in there, and the second one was that when Grandma told us to stay away from Grandpa's den because he needed time to "think," we knew she was "lyin'" to us. Grandpa was drinking in there.

Now Grandma had no patience with a man who was drinking, but she seemed to be able to make an allowance for it if Grandpa stayed put in his Den. Of course, I was almost ten before I figured that out, and when I tried to ask Grandma about it, I got my ears boxed good. She told me little boys should worry about little boy things and let the adults take care of adult things.

I have noticed when as an adult, we tell a child something like that, we seldom finish the statement with "Now at the age of blah blah blah, you are old enough to ask that stuff." Perhaps that is why they just shake their heads and do what they want to when spoken to by an a-dult. "Dult" defined in the Urban Dictionary is "a deliberately dumb or dull insult, used when replying to someone who said or wrote something stupid or insipid."

It seemed appropriate for me to say something stupid now, so I shout into the empty room, "If you are in here, show yourself," which was probably not necessary as the room was, as I stated, "empty." What a "dult" thing to say.

I glance around the Den, shiver for no apparent reason, and walk right back out into the dining room. I stand there for a moment, deciding on my next move, and I hear a car door shut. Then I realize the only vehicle out here is my truck.

I run for the front door, burst out of it, and see that my truck has not moved even though the keys are in the ignition. The passenger door is open and so is the glovebox door, and its contents have clearly been gone through. I lean in and do a quick inventory—everything is intact.

I lean back to step away from the door of the truck and feel an explosion on the back of my head. I see a flash of light as I fall backwards. When I come to, I see that flash of light again as I open my eyes and realize I am looking straight up at the sun. Dang, my head hurts. Dang, my pride hurts.

As I lay on the ground next to my truck, and my head slowly clears, I look at my watch. I have been out for about fifteen minutes. As I get to my knees and grab the door handle to pull myself up, I see my keys are now gone. The plot thickens.

Slowly I turn and look at the house. *Houses are not living things*, I tell myself, but I swear the house is laughing at me. I have never done well when being laughed at. I stare at the house and ask it what it is laughing at. The house is unresponsive to my request for an answer, so I turn my back to it in disdain.

My head hurts, but I can think now. I look for tracks other than mine, hoping to get an idea about my attacker. I am not disappointed as I find boot tracks behind where I was standing. They are man-sized and look to be the kind of tread that was on the boots we wore when we were out in the swampy areas of the property.

I go into tracking mode and follow the boot prints toward the pond. When I was a young, Joseph's father taught me how to track the animals that lived on our property. He did not hunt, but he loved the outdoors and everything that lived there. We would spend hours tracking an animal just to look at it when we located it. At the time, it seemed pointless to my young mind. I realized later in life that the tracking was part of "the lesson" I was learning about "myself "as much as I was learning how to track.

"Patience, perseverance, purpose," he told me. I could use those three right now. My attacker seems headed toward the swampy area just south of the pond. I am cautious as I followed the tracks around the edge of the pond, all my senses on high alert to prevent another blindside attack. Now that adrenaline has kicked in, my head was clear, and my purpose was also. I would not be the prey, I must become the predator. This lion was out of the den!

CHAPTER 4

Joseph and Jerry

As I track and search for my attacker, my mind wanders back to Joseph. As far as I know, he is the only one who knew I was coming. I had called Joseph a couple of weeks ago to make sure the key was in place and gave him an expected arrival date. He did not know I would be three days earlier than that date though.

Joseph is just a name to you at this point, but he is the son of my grandparents' "right-hand" man, Jerry. Jerry McDougal was the overseer of all the plantation. He was the eyes and ears of this place for Grandma and Grandpa. His family immigrated here from Ireland around 1800s. He had a heavy accent, but I found it very pleasing to listen to. When he got excited, it was hard for most people to understand him, but I could always decipher his rough English. He was a man's man, have no doubt. My father taught me to be a gentleman, and Jerry taught me patience and how to fight after my father passed away.

Ah yes, my father. We shall discuss him later. He was a great man himself but only here with me for a short time. I loved him dearly and still miss him.

Now back to Jerry and Joseph and the task at hand. Joseph was an odd child, very quiet and very angry. Joseph is five years younger than me and hated the relationship I had with his father. My father died in a farm accident when I was thirteen, my brother was nine, and Joseph was eight. I was mired in grief for about six months when Jerry finally got me to go tracking with him.

On the morning after Dad was killed, I was hiding in my room grieving when Grandma came in and told me I was to go with Jerry. I did not want to go, but Grandma made me, and talking back to grandma was not permitted. I grudgingly put on my boots and joined him on the back porch. We started looking for tracks in the exact area I was in now. It seems that every square inch of this place holds a memory or a reflection of one.

Speaking of reflections, I find the last of the boot prints at the edge of the swamp on the south side of the pond. I peer into the water's edge and see my own face looking back at me. There is blood in my hair and mud on the side of my face. I look disheveled and like I lost a fight. My clothes are dirty, and my boots are a mess. I can see that I will track no further, and I decide to go back to my truck and get some clean clothes. There is a well at the house that I hope still pumps, and I will clean up and change. I need a fresh outlook and a chance to think this situation through.

As I head back to the house, I think again about only Joseph knowing I was coming, but no one knew I was coming three days early. As much as he hated me as a child, I think Joseph and I had made our peace long ago.

On the other hand, he was five years younger than me, and at the ages we were now, that five years was an advantage, not a disadvantage. He hated me, but he did love the plantation. This was his home most of his life. The day we shut it down, I remember Joseph just standing and staring out across the pond. I walked up to him to talk, and he had the old Polaroid camera in his hand that Grandpa had given to Jerry years ago. I asked him what he was doing, he told me I would never understand, and he walked away.

My keyless truck is still here and so is my travel duffel. I rummage through it and find some clothes. My Glock is in the holster and locked up in its lock box, but I choose to leave it for now. I get in the back under the tonto cover and get out my swamp boots. I will most likely be needing them.

Good news, the old pump still works, but the water is freezing cold as I wash up. I have a distinct feeling I am being watched. I look around but see no one. Perseverance, patience, purpose. The mind is now calm, and my initial shock and agitation are giving way to determination.

I make my way back to the truck and pop the hood. I am going to make it hard to take the truck even with the keys. With the tools I have in my truck, I remove the battery cables and a few sparkplug wires. If someone wants to take the truck now, it will take some parts and work to do so. I put the parts in my duffle and start looking for a place to hide it.

It seems to me it is time to go back to the barn. As I cross the yard to the barn, it seemed to have taken on a new ominous look. It does not seem at all inviting but more like it is daring me to come in. I have developed an innate ability to see life in inanimate objects, and I'm in continued conversation with them. They never speak but are constantly talking to me. In my line of work, everything I see is saying something. How good I am at what I do is based on how well I listen.

I am eyes wide open as I head for the barn.

CHAPTER 5

The Barn

The barn is still in the same place. It would have not bothered me if it was not there when I got back to it. The "barn" holds some great memories for me, but one bad one that lays at the edge of my conscious mind always.

As a child growing up, my brother and I played in the barn all the time. If it was raining, the barn was our haven to get out of the old house. The haymow was our favorite place to play. We built forts out of the bales and tunnels to other worlds. Our imagination could take us far from the plantation without leaving the property. We were always fighting, but you had better not pick on either one of us or the other one would put some welts on you. That's what we used to say to each other when we threatened to beat each other up, and that's what Grandma would say to us when we got in trouble: "I am going to put some welts on you boys." And we would run to the barn and hide. Of course, it did not matter to Grandma because she knew we would be back in eventually. Then the welt putting on would commence. You never got out of punishment when it came to Grandma.

Now Grandpa was a different story. I think we reminded him of himself when he was a young boy, so he tended to yell at us and wink, then warn us not to do it again or Grandma would put some welts on us.

We were a little scared of Grandpa and never really knew why. I think Grandpa knew that and tried to show us we did not need to be, but there was a sense we both had that he was hiding something, and we could never get quite at ease with him. I found it easier to be with Jerry than Grandpa. When I asked Jerry about Grandpa, he would always say to me that I should leave him well enough alone. That really did not make me feel any better, by the way.

Obviously, Jerry knew something, but the information was closely guarded. I suppose that is why Grandpa trusted Jerry like he did. Now Grandma did not have the same trust for Jerry that Grandpa did, and every now and then we would hear her voice that opinion. Later in life, I would find out why that was.

Once again, I went on a rabbit trail with my thoughts so here we are, entering the barn. The side door I had entered through earlier was still hanging open so that was my point of entry into the jaws of the "barn." All the stalls are of course empty now. There are no longer horses in this barn to whinny in search of an apple or sugar as I enter. I look up at the haymows, and they are also empty. There will be no fort-building today through a tunnel to another world sounds inviting.

I start out by looking for footprints in the dust on the barn floor and see no sign of any at this point. I am sure I saw someone or something by the barn earlier. There should be prints here. I am a man of reason, so I ask myself if there is any good reason for all of this to be happening, and better yet is there any good reason for me to stay here? The answer to both questions is yes, so I refocus and move on into the barn further.

I think I see some movement up in the rafters, and as my eyes adjust to the light, there is an explosion of flapping as a flock of pigeons exit the barn through one of the broken haymow windows, breaking the deafening silence of the moment and making my heart pound in my chest. As I bring my attention back down to the lower portion of the barn, I notice that there are tire tracks coming in and exiting the sliding barn doors up ahead of me.

As I move toward them, I also see footprints around the tire tracks. I move to examine this area and see that this activity has been recent as there is still some moisture in the tire tracks. As I am examining the tracks, I see the outline of a trap door in the dirt. The door leads to the cellar under the barn. As children, we were not allowed to play in the cellar, and it was kept padlocked.

The padlock is gone, and I am not a child anymore.

I survey the barn quickly and prepare to open the trap door. *What will I find?* I wonder as I stand at the door and grab the old handle.

I pull on it and remember the door to be quite heavy. I put my back into it and try again. It opens slowly, and I move with it to flop it all the way open. I let go of it, and it falls backward and slams into the dirt floor with a resounding thud. I think to myself, *There is no doubt that my adversary knows where I am now.*

I can see the first few steps, but it is pitch black down below them. The power is off so the light switch, which must have been added long after the barn was erected, does not turn the light on. That did not keep me from trying the switch, however.

When you are considering going into the jaws of darkness, into a place you don't want to go, a little wishful thinking is unavoidable. Grandpa used to say, "Wish in one hand and well, you know what in the other and see which one gets full first." It used to be funny. Not so much right now.

I decide that I must go back to my truck and get my flashlight if I am to enter the bowels of the barn. I laugh at myself for that thought because I really am in some crap here. This trip down memory lane is really going south on me. I am reasonably calm at this point and head back out of the barn to my truck, hoping the flashlight is there

As I step out of the side barn door and back into the sunlight, I hear a mocking bird singing and think to myself, *How appropriate.*

I head to the truck. The flashlight is there, I grab it and head back to the barn. The cellar beckons, I heed the call.

CHAPTER 6

Into the Darkness

I make my way back to the barn and prepare myself to enter the cellar. My mind goes back to a day many years ago. As I told you earlier, "the barn" has many great memories but also that one significant bad one. It has steamrolled to the front of my mind and though I have repressed it for years, I seem unable to do that now and though I am not yet to the cellar, I step into "the darkness."

Jerry had a brother-in-law named William Smith who was a ne'er-do-well sort of fellow. My grandfather hired "Smitty" as a favor to Jerry. Smitty was often at odds with the law and "the truth" for that matter. He was not the kind of fellow that most people would give a chance to, but as I told you, Jerry was protecting Grandpa, and Grandpa was a man who honored a debt—even a hidden one.

Grandpa hired Smitty to help Jerry. You could pretty much always find Jerry hard at work and Smitty resting and smoking, watching Jerry work. He used to say that just watching Jerry work wore him out. I am relatively sure that that was one of the few times he told the truth.

Smitty loved to drink, and he loved the women. He was not very good at either. Smitty was not a good-looking man, and the two broken noses he had received in his life had left him with a very crooked nose. That did seem appropriate though. Grandma used to say that Smitty was so crooked that he could not walk a straight line.

Jerry's wife Esther, however, loved her little brother, and she was quite blind to the fact that her sibling seemed unable to just do the right thing, no matter how small. Smitty liked to go down into the cellar in the barn in the heat of the day and drink because it was always cool down there. The humid heat of our area in the middle and late part of summer was almost unbearable if you had to work out in it. Of course, Smitty did anything he could to avoid work and all the unpleasant side effects of it.

One late July afternoon, we were just getting back to the barn with a load of hay from the field, and we heard muffled shouting and swearing. At first, we could not discern where it was coming from. After a moment of listening, Jerry shouted, "It is coming from the cellar!"

We all ran into the barn just as we heard the first shot fired. That sound stopped us dead in our tracks. Jerry told us to wait, and he would go down by himself. Grandpa tried to stop him but to no avail. The cellar door was open, and as Jerry took the first step, we heard the second gunshot and the scream of a woman. Jerry took a breath and ran down the steps.

We all moved toward the doorway and heard Jerry say, "Oh my word, Wilma, what happened here?"

We looked at one another, and the resounding silence was shattered by another gunshot. This time, Grandpa was not to be held back, and he took the stairs two at a time and disappeared into the cellar. That just left me Joseph and my brother at the top.

Grandpa hollered up at us, "Do not come down here boys!"

We looked at one another and crept down the steps.

There is a point in the descent to the cellar where the light does not illuminate the room until you clear the actual ceiling of the cellar in relationship to the stairs. It was at that point that the scene came into full view. Joseph, my brother, and I stopped, and our world was forever changed.

There was blood everywhere. I counted three bodies in the room and a close-range gunshot wound to the head is not like on TV. The back of Smitty's skull was on the wall behind him. Wilma's face was destroyed, and her husband Sam had a huge hole in his chest.

Grandpa saw us and pushed us back up the stairs and told us to go tell Grandma to call the sheriff and to stay out of the barn. We ran to the house in shock. By the time the sheriff got there, we were all in the barnyard trying to console Esther to no avail and still in shock about the mess in the cellar.

Sheriff Buck Branson was a good man who knew his county and the people in it. Sheriff Branson was quite young for a county sheriff. He was a deputy when his father Sheriff Tom Branson was killed when he answered a domestic dispute call. The mayor made Buck the acting sheriff because the election was only a few months away. Buck did a good job, and when he decided to run, his only opponent was a deputy ready for retirement. He won, and here he was. Buck grew up here, and he was destined to be a law man just like his daddy. He might be young, but he was well-liked and well-respected.

He arrived with the Coroner Bill Potts and took a few moments to check on all of us before he went down to the scene. After asking us if we had moved anything or messed with the scene, he told us to stay out of the barn and let them do their jobs. Jerry said he had checked all three bodies for a pulse and that he had not moved them. He also asked if anyone had touched the gun, and we all said no. The sheriff and the coroner moved into the cellar and left us alone with our questions and grief.

I watched as Joseph quietly slipped away from everyone and headed for the pond. I excused myself from the group to Grandma's concern about where I was going and followed Joseph from a distance. He seemed to be in no hurry as he walked aimlessly with his head down, kicking rocks and talking to himself under his breath. I strained to hear him, but I could not. If I risked getting closer, I figured he would pick up on my presence, but he seemed unaware of anyone or anything as he moved along.

He soon reached the pond and stopped by the edge. Without turning, he said, "You may as well come on up here. I know you have been following me."

Without speaking, I moved up beside him. We stood together in silence for a while, pretending to look at the water. Joseph finally spoke, and what he said was unexpected and hard for a boy his age. "He got what he deserved."

I looked at him in surprise and asked, "Do you mean Smitty?" and he said "Yes."

I asked him, "Why would you say that?"

He surprised me again when he said, "He has been sleeping with her for weeks." I was dumfounded. How could this be? And no one know but Joseph. In my heart, I wondered if there were others who knew. Could this mess have been avoided?

I asked him if he was going to tell anyone, and he said no way, and if I said he had told me, he would say I was lying. When I told him all the reasons he should speak up, he told me, "You didn't know anything about my world, and you should mind your own business." With that. he turned and ran back toward the house.

I was left standing by the pond, watching the sun set on the day and on three people's lives. As the sunny day turned into night on the Carolina coast, a darkness settled on my soul.

CHAPTER 7

The Cellar

I slowly swim back up out of the memory and look around myself. Everything seems to be the way I left it when I took my walk down memory lane. I find I have only moved a few feet away from my truck. The flashlight is still in my hand, and I force myself to move toward the barn.

As I prepare to enter the barn, I notice the footprints of a dog that I had missed before. I kneeled and look closer at them, and they seem almost familiar to me. As I stand back up, I realize that I am squeezing the hatchet hard enough to leave fingerprints, and somehow, the flashlight is already turned on. I file the dog footprints in the "think about later" category and move into the barn.

The flashlight sends a faint beam across the expanse of the barn having the same effect that a ray of sunlight does. There are thousands of tiny specks of dust suspended in the air. It is like a picture of the stars in outer space but reversed. In space, the background is the darkness, and the stars are lit. In this scene, the stars are the darkness, and the background is lit. It seems to me that this paradox of reversal is becoming a common theme for me on this return to the plantation.

I am a man used to being on offense, not defense. It is obvious to me that the plantation has new secrets to reveal. My life has been dedicated to the uncovering of the truth, so I shift myself back into work mode and go on the offense.

When I reach the cellar door, I take a closer look at the tire tracks and the footprints. The tire tracks are from a tread I have seen before, but I can't seem to recall the brand. I do know that it is from a newer design of tire. The footprints are the same type of boot as the prints of my attacker but two different sizes. It appears there were two people here, and they were going up and down the stairs to the cellar.

I shine the light down the steps and over the whole entrance area, looking for any type of trap or trip wire device. That may sound paranoid to you, but in my profession, I have learned that caution and attention to every little detail or variation might save my life. This whole situation reeks of danger, and I am getting bad vibes from the evidence I have seen so far—especially the part where I got knocked out. I do not intend for that to happen again, and I proceed with caution down the steps.

As I reach that point on the steps where my flashlight can survey the lower area of the cellar, I sweep the beam slowly over the room. I can see where there were crates sitting on the floor. But the cellar is empty now. I start to move into the cellar when I hear a noise upstairs in the barn, and I realize how precarious my position is down here.

I race up the stairs, and when I get to the top, I see the barn door go shut. I run for the door and fling it open, but there is no one in sight. The cellar did not answer many questions but has gave me much to think about. I had hoped I would not need it, but I think it is time to get my Glock out of my duffel bag. There is something going on, and someone does not want me here.

Calm mind, I tell myself. *Get your gun, John.*

CHAPTER 8

Where'd You Get "the Gun," John?

I guess it is time I introduce myself to you. My name is John. Retired Sheriff John Young. This is how I got "the gun."

It all started that day in the cellar. Over the next few days after the shootings, I watched Sheriff Branson go through the steps of his investigation, and I was intrigued by the process. I tried to stay as close to him as I could during his time on the farm as he questioned all of us and gathered evidence.

The sheriff stopped me one day and said, "Why don't you and I take a walk and have a little talk, John?"

The sheriff was a big man, and I felt quite small by his side as we walked together. He said, "I have been watching you, son, and you seem to have quite an interest in this investigation. Is there any particular reason for your interest you would like to share with me?"

I considered his knowing eyes and felt like he was considering my soul. In the years to follow, I would see that characteristic in all good lawmen. I am sure at some point in your life, you have looked into the eyes of someone who asked you a question, and you knew you could not lie. That was me then.

I told the sheriff what Joseph had told me by the pond and that he would say I was lying if I told anyone. I then shared with the sheriff that I was considering a future in law enforcement, and his handling of the investigation was intriguing to me.

He laughed and told me to keep in mind I would not get rich, but I would get tired, insulted, and lonely. I laughed and told him that I had been in training for that position for years. He smiled and said, "Come along with me, John," and we headed back toward the barn.

As we walked, he asked me if I knew how my family had grown to be wealthy. I responded, "With hard work and sweat."

He laughed heartily and said, "Who told you that, son?"

I said, "Grandma."

He just smiled and kept on walking. I followed close behind, wandering at his remarks.

When we got near the barn, we saw Grandpa getting off the old John Deere, and he came walking toward us. We stopped, and as he approached, he asked the sheriff, "Is the boy bothering you, sheriff?"

The sheriff answered, "No, he is not, Paul. John and I are having a talk. You know what the boy told me, Paul? He said your wife Martha told him your family built its wealth with hard work and sweat."

Grandpa looked at the sheriff like a deer in the headlights of an oncoming truck and said nothing. I stood, waiting for some type of revelation, but all I got was "You boys keep doing what you're doing," and Grandpa turned and headed back to the old John Deere. He got up on it, fired it up, and off he went.

The sheriff did not say a word and started walking on toward the barn. I followed, expecting to be told to move on, but he said not a word. As the sheriff opened the door to the barn, he turned and told me to go to his squad car and get his flashlight. He said, "It is on the front seat, John."

As I turned to go, he said, "Just a moment, John, you will need these," and tossed me his keys. He turned and headed into the barn. I felt quite important as I ran to his squad car. When I got to the car, I found the key that fit the lock and unlocked the door to my future.

Of course, I did not know that my life was forever changed. Once again, we see the significance of the word *key*.

When I got back to the barn, the sheriff was standing at the top of the cellar stairs, waiting. I handed him his flashlight and the keys, he nodded his thank you, and then he told me to wait at the top while he went down. He lifted the crime scene tape and started down the steps.

I pleaded with him to come along, but I got a firm "no," and down he went. I stood quietly, wondering what he was doing down there, and waited. He was only gone a few minutes, and when he returned, he was carrying a bag marked "evidence."

The sheriff lifted the crime scene tape and stepped back into the barn from the cellar. He closed the cellar door with a loud bang and started toward the barn door. I stood there, wanting to ask him what was going on, but no words would come out of my mouth.

He turned, looked back at me, and said, "Are you coming, John?"

I said, "Yes, sir," and followed him out of the barn. Once again, I felt small but somehow not quite as small. This was to be the beginning of a lifelong friendship. The sheriff stopped at the house and asked Grandma if I could go with him for the day. Grandma fussed for a little bit about my safety and then said okay. She turned to me and sternly said, "Don't get into any mischief, John," and gave me her blessing to leave.

That day, I did just that. I left. I left behind childish things and immersed myself even further into "the lesson". Most of the day, I listened and watched as the sheriff went through his daily routine. As I look back on that day now, I remember how enthralled I was with the way the sheriff carried himself and the way he interacted with the people he came into contact with. I found myself taking on his demeanor even at my young age. The kids in school got to calling me "deputy." I was not offended by it at all. I was quite happy to be called "deputy." My path was set. My mind was made up.

Grandma used to say, "When a man from the Young family made his mind up, there was no changing it." I believe she was correct. I have been called stubborn over the years, but I prefer to be called John.

CHAPTER 9

Tick Glock and Dixie Too

Time is a-wasting. I go to the truck and get my gun and holster out of the gun safe behind the seat. Glock in hand, I decide on my next move. I did not pay much attention when I pulled onto the property this morning, so I decide to walk back to the entrance and inspect the driveway from the gate on up to the farmhouse.

As I make my way back, I now see the evidence of traffic coming and going that I had not noticed before. When I get to the gate, I see that the hinges are not rusted up like they should be. Someone has oiled them. I look up at the sun and note that I have wasted a lot of time. The sun is moving far too quickly across the sky, and the day is going to turn to night way too soon.

I follow the tracks back to the farm house, and they go right where I thought they would—to the barn door. I can see evidence that the vehicle pulled forward and backed up to the barn door. Someone then got out and opened the padlocked door and the tracks go under the door. A padlock that I don't have a key for is guarding the barn door. There is, however, a bolt cutter in my tools in the truck. That is a tool I used quite often in my sheriff duties. I have been on the other side of this door already, so I am in no hurry to cut the padlock.

I decide to walk the area around the entrance of the barn and look for any other evidence that might be about. As I survey the area, I notice a cigarette butt in the edge of the grass by the drive. I bend over and pick it up with my hanky and see that it is a Camel, unfiltered. In my memory, I know someone who smoked that brand, and it is right there but won't come to me at this moment.

The cigarette butt in hand, my mind wanders down a memory path as it often does. I am standing by the barn about a week after the mess in the cellar and I notice Joseph over in the apple grove by himself and it looks to me like he is smoking.

I walk over and surprise him, but he does not even flinch. I ask him, "Aren't you afraid you will get caught?" and he responds, "Who cares."

I ask him, "Where did you get the cigarettes?" and he says, "I stole them," quite matter-of-factly. He then says to me, "You even act like a cop," and he walked away.

As the memory comes to life in my mind, I see the cigarette pack in his hand as he put it in his shirt pocket. He was smoking a Camel non-filter that day. I come back to the present and ponder the revelation. I store the information on the hard drive of my memory and continue to search then area.

I decide to use a circular search pattern with the barn as the epicenter. I move out about ten feet and start my first circle around the barn. All if my senses are on high alert as I move slowly around the barn. I finish my first pass with no new evidence, and I move out ten more feet and start the second pass. About half way around the barn, on the back side in the bushes, I see movement.

I quickly pull my Glock and go into a shooting stance. I wait motionless as the bushes part and out walks "Dixie." But of course, it can't be Dixie. My first dog Dixie has been gone for years and years.

I am in a state of denial for a moment, wanting it to be Dixie but of course that is not possible. I loved that dog. I holster my gun and drop to one knee and start coaxing the dog to come to me. It appears to be a female, so I offer my coaxing addressing the dog in the female vernacular.

"Come here, girl," I softly coax.

She is hesitant but moves toward me. I pull some jerky out of my pocket and offer it to her, and she comes to me with her tail tucked. I hold out the jerky, and she gently takes it from my hand, backs up, and looks at me as if asking for permission to eat it.

I say, "Go ahead, girl, eat it," and she wolfs it down. As I move slowly toward her, she looks up at me with fear in her eyes, so I continue to talk to her and tell her she is safe and I won't hurt her.

I ask her, "What's your name, girl?"

She tilts her head as if to say, "Silly man, I can't talk." I laugh at myself and say to her, "So I guess that means you won't tell my why you are here either?"

At that moment, her tail comes up, and she starts to wag it. I smile and say, "Come here, girl," and she moves toward me. Suddenly I am fourteen years old and in the swamp with Jerry on one of our tracking expeditions.

As Jerry and I quietly make our way around the pond, we hear a whining coming from a thicket some distance up a small creek that feeds the pond. We move toward the sound and what we find makes us both furious. We find a dog covered in mud and blood in an animal trap. Everyone in our area knows we do not allow trapping.

We move toward the badly hurt dog to see if we can possibly save it or if we will have to put it out of its misery. As soon as I get close, I see its eyes. My heart is gone. The dog lets us remove the trap as it whines in pain, and I beg Jerry to bring it home so I can see if Grandma can help it. When we get back to the house, Grandma is hanging clothes on the line.

As we approach her, she turns and asks, "What are you dragging home, John?" I tell her the story, and she is mad as an old wet hen. She says, "Let me look at that critter!"

As she examines the dog, she sends me for a bucket of warm water and rags. When I get back, Grandma and Jerry have the dog up on a horse blanket on the picnic table. Grandma proceeds to clean the dog up and inspects the broken leg.

As Grandma gets her cleaned up, I see that she is a red ginger color and reminds me of pictures that I saw in school of the Australian Dingo. Once again, I get dragged in by those eyes. They are no longer the sad eyes of an animal in pain, they are inquisitive and intelligent, and she seemed to be deciding something. In my heart, I knew what she was deciding. She was deciding if I was the one. I looked into her eyes and said "Yes. You are mine, and I am yours."

Grandma looked at me and said, "Okay, boy, let's save your dog." Grandma was smart and tough, but she recognized love at first sight. Years later, she told me with a smile in her voice, "Your Grandpa looked at me the same way the day we met," and she laughed. It was unusual for Grandma to laugh, and it made me smile.

Dixie and I were inseparable from that day on. Within a few days, she was up and walking with her homemade splint Grandma made after setting the leg, and within a few months, she was running and jumping as if nothing had happened. I made a promise to God that if he helped Dixie get better, I would help him.

I never told anyone about that promise because I thought they would say, "God does not need your help." As I matured into a man, I realized that he might not need it, but that he wanted it. It was all a part of "the lesson."

CHAPTER 10

The Partner

I come back from the memory and find this new dog standing by me, looking up at me as if to say, "What do we do next?" I bend down and pet her and see that same look in her eyes that Dixie gave me years ago, and my heart was gone again.

I check her for any kind of tags or identification and find nothing. I say, "Okay, let's go, girl," and she falls in beside me. As I resume the search with my new partner in tow, she seems to sense her place in the search and starts to move a little further out from me in the search pattern, as if to say, "Okay, John, we can cover more ground if we spread out." I laugh at myself for making such an assumption and get back to the business at hand.

We were just finishing the last twenty feet of the search orbit, and "Dixie" stops and starts to whine. I quickly move over to where she is standing and look down to see a glove lying on the ground. I pick it up with a stick and proceed to visually examine it. I instantly come to two conclusions: one, there is what appears to be dried blood on this glove; two, I just called the dog Dixie in my mind.

I reminded myself there could be numerous reasons for blood on a work glove such as this one. There is, of course, the obvious question of why was anyone even on the property? This place has been closed up for years.

I give the dog the last of my jerky, which she wolfs down, and use the empty bag to pocket the work glove. I tell the dog "Good girl," for which I receive a dog smile, and we continue the search. She falls into the same pattern with me again, and we resume the search orbit, slowly working our way closer and closer to the pond. We have been on the hunt now for about an hour and have uncovered nothing of significance. I determine we should head back to the barn, and we make our way back cautiously.

The feeling of familiarity with this dog is almost spooky. She looks amazingly like Dixie, and her mannerisms are eerily similar. For years, Dixie and I walked this property together, and my grandpa would always call her my partner. I had that same feeling now. I stopped and knelt down, and she came right to me as if to say, "It's okay, John, I am here now."

I rubbed her head with one hand on each side, just like I used to Dixie, and she smiled again. I stopped and stood up and got a "woof" from her as if to say, "Why did you stop?" and I said, "Let's go, girl." She moved in ahead of me like Dixie always did and led the way, constantly sniffing the ground and air as if to say, "Follow me, John." So that is what I did: I followed her.

My new partner led me back around the barn and back toward the pond. As we worked our way past my truck, I wondered where she was leading me. Frankly, I did not care. Now that I have an alarm system if anyone approaches, my mind wonders again back to another Dixie memory.

One day as I was fishing in the pond with Dixie exploring but staying in close proximity to me, I heard her give her "Hey, John" woof. I looked up to see Joseph standing off in the bushes, staring at Dixie. He had an ugly scowl on his face.

I watched him for a little bit before he realized I was watching him stare at my dog. Suddenly I felt very possessive of Dixie. Joseph was looking at her like a hunter looks at his prey, and I did not like it. He felt my stare and looked at me with disdain and said something I will never forget: "That damned dog should have died in my trap."

I stood and said, "Are you are telling me that you set the trap that Dixie was caught in?"

He smiled broadly and answered, "Yes."

I dropped my fishing pole and ran at him. I caught him with a right cross flush on the left cheek and knocked him down hard. He looked up at me as his head cleared and smiled through his bloody teeth. "You can't hurt me."

I said, "We will see about that," and reached down to pull him up for his beating just as Grandpa came up on the tractor. He asked, "What is going on here?" and Joseph quickly said, "I fell, and John is helping me up. Grandpa knowingly nodded his head and moved on.

I asked Joseph why he would say that, and he said, "Because this is between you and me." I agreed and hit him again. As I walked away, he whispered, "This is not over".

I answered, "You are right," and headed toward him to punch him, but he got up and ran. As you might guess, my relationship with Joseph was to say the least strained from that day on. Okay, *strained* is not the right word. I hated him for what he had done, but most of all. I hated him for his lack of remorse.

As "the lesson" continued to flow through my life, I eventually had to forgive Joseph. My Father taught me when I was quite young that hate is a cancer that festers in a man's soul and holding onto it is like taking poison and expecting it to hurt someone else. Though I forgave Joseph, I would never trust him again. Little did I know at that point in our young lives that it was hate blossoming from hurt that was tearing Joseph apart inside.

I snap back to the present and realize I have been standing in one spot for quite a while. My new Dixie is sitting beside me, looking up at me quizzically. I reach down scratch between her ears and say to her, "Life is an adventure, girl. 'The lesson' continues. Lead on, girl. What the heck. Lead on, Dixie!"

We were soon back to the house and I saw the old porch swing was sitting under the porch overhang and although the chains were rusty, it still looked to be in usable condition. As a child and a young man, I watched many a sunset and rainstorm from that swing. I decided to try and rehang it, and after a little wrestling, I had it back up.

I cautiously set myself down and waited for it to give way, but it held me. I went back to the truck and got some WD40 and sprayed the chains down and took a seat again to begin to think on my next move as Dixie takes her place on the porch beside me. I return to my thoughts of Joseph and how he must fit into the events of this day. I am recalling what my grandpa told me on his deathbed about Joseph's father. That conversation is running through my mind when the kind of silence filled with the sounds of nature is shattered by a gun shot.

Dixie and I jump to our feet on high alert. Most dogs would have barked, but Dixie just gives a soft "woof "and looks at me. The sound seems to have come from the woods behind the barn. I pull the Glock and move cautiously toward the barn. Dixie is slightly in front of me, sniffing the air and ground with her ears up. If you were to research the Carolina dog history, you would find they are a very intelligent breed of dog, and it is apparent right now that she has an understanding that this is a dangerous situation.

My partner and I move toward the area I believe the shot to have come from. I am in sheriff mode now.

CHAPTER 11

More Questions

I hear the sound of an ATV starting and pick my speed up to a cautious jog. It seems to labor a moment, and then I hear it moving away from us quickly, so I start to run.

About a hundred yards into the woods, I find a clearing and smell gunpowder. I stop and survey the area. It is clear there was a struggle here. I see blood on the ground, and it is apparent someone was dragged a short distance. The drag marks end where the tire marks start. Clearly the ATV pulled up and stopped here, then moved on again and quickly. The tire tracks tell me that the ATV was heavier when it left than when it arrived. From this, I must conclude that a second person was added to the ATV, presumably the one who was bleeding. I decide to scour the area for footprints.

Glock still at the ready, we slowly survey the area. There are two sets of footprints. There is a fresh set of tracks coming from the ocean side of the property, but all around them, I see old tracks, and as I follow them toward the ocean, it is obvious that this trek was used many times before. The ATV tire tracks follow the same trekked area toward the ocean, which is about a half mile away. I can no longer hear the ATV so chasing after it would serve no purpose.

I tell Dixie, "Let's go," and we head toward the ocean. I keep the Glock in hand and wish I had a bottle of water as we head toward the beach. We proceed at a cautious yet steady pace, and it is not long before I hear the waves crashing on the beach.

My family's property lay along a quite rugged area of the Carolina shoreline, with the exception of one beautiful but small cove. The water is deep blue, and the sand is white as snow. The cove is deep and well-hidden. When we were children and later young adults, this was a spot we could come and be oblivious to the world. When we were children, my father would bring my brother and I here for family outings.

One of my favorite memories is the Christmas Eve we spent here, the night lit only by the moon and a raging bonfire. It was mild weather that night, and we bundled up and sang Christmas carols and drank eggnog, ate pie and candy as we laughed, and then Dad told stories by the firelight. At the end of the night, I felt as close to my family as I ever had in my life. At that moment, I wondered how Christmas could possibly top this night.

It didn't. Christmas day was cloudy, dark and wet. A storm blew in off of the ocean and blew through our lives as the beauty of the night was erased by the sunless day.

Dixie and I move out of the brush along the beachline and onto the beach.

It is just as beautiful as I remember. I do a quick visual sweep of the area and see no one or anything is on the beach. I can, however, see where a boat has recently beached and footprints all around it. The ATV tracks go down to where the boat was beached and then take off south along the beach. I stop and gaze out over the bay and recall something my grandma said to me: if anyone ever tells you, "You are not the sharpest tack in the box," remember you are still a tack.

I laugh to myself and think, *Okay, let's get to the point*, and laugh again. I amuse myself easily. I spend a lot of time alone, and I am relatively sure I am funny. Or so I say. To myself.

Back to the situation at hand. All of the clues to this point would indicate that something illegal is going on here. I have never been knocked out to cover a humanitarian effort. I think I need to go back to the barn and inspect that cellar more closely. Patience, perseverance, purpose. Calm mind. "The lesson" continues but with more questions to answer.

CHAPTER 12

The Cellar: Revisited

As Dixie and I head back to the barn, I suddenly realize that Dixie never barked through this whole episode. Kind of odd. I stop, kneel down, and she comes up to me with a quizzical look on her face. It would seem to me that she is not used to receiving affection.

I take her face in my hands and say, "If only you could talk, you could answer most of my questions." She gives me that dog smile as though to say, "Yep, you are correct," but I am pretty sure she just likes the attention.

I say, "Let's pick up the pace, girl," and off we go. It is a fairly long walk back to the barn, so I allow my mind to wander as Dixie is now on duty.

Grandpa and I were in the barn cellar getting apples for Christmas dinner on Christmas morning, and Dad was right outside the barn running the log splitter. Though it was a dreary day, Grandpa was in rare humor as we worked, and he was in a storytelling mood.

He asked me, "John, have I ever told you about the day I met your grandma?"

I answered no, and he said, "Now Grandma might not tell it like this, but this is how it happened." Before he could start the story, we heard Grandma at the top of the cellar, yelling for Grandpa to get up there right away. Wendall was hurt badly.

Wendall was my dad's name!

Grandpa took the steps two at a time, and I was right behind him. Grandma tried to stop me, but I was having none of that, and I avoided her grasp and followed Grandpa to where Dad was splitting wood. Dad was on the ground bleeding badly from his head, and the ram on the log splitter was broken and bent.

Grandpa bent over Dad and tore his shirt off and tried to use it to stop the bleeding, but the wound was very deep, and there seemed to be no slowing the flow of blood. Grandma ran to the house to call for help, but by the time the ambulance got there, followed by the sheriff, it was too late. My dad was gone. Merry Christmas, John.

My little brother Ron had come out of the house by this time and was in Grandma's arms, balling. I was standing by Grandpa who was looking at the blood on his hands like he did not understand how it got there when Sheriff Branson walked over and put his big hand on my shoulder. He said, "John, come with me." I followed him in a daze.

He asked me, "Are you okay, John?"

I answered him, "Yes sir," and he said, "Tell me what you know to this point."

As we spoke, I began to see that this was part of "the lesson." I needed step aside from my emotion and look at the facts. Grieving would come, but today's event would change me again and quickly. My view of life changed that day. I saw life for what it was—a precious, simple but complex gift to be cherished and shared. The promise does not even include today.

I came to understand later in life that I could have taken a completely different path as a result of the death of my father—one of anger and self-pity, one leading to addiction and self-destruction. The sheriff had lost his father at a young age also. His guidance would be a saving grace in my future. Life can be taken in a moment.

I was in shock, and the sheriff knew it. He said, "John, I want you to go be with your family. The EMS people and I will take care of your dad. Now get along to the house."

I answered him "Yes sir," and headed for the house. It was a lonely walk, that walk you take after you examine a dead body—a walk I would take many more times in my life.

CHAPTER 13

There Is a New Sheriff in Town

Dixie and I make our way back to the house and up the steps onto the porch. I look at the old swing and gingerly take a seat on it. It creaks again but holds me, and I reflect on the day so far. I am settling into my analytical sheriff mindset when I hear a vehicle coming up the drive. It is not in sight yet, so I move quickly around the side of the house Dixie in tow, conceal myself, and wait.

It is just a few moments, and I catch sight of the SUV. It is a county sheriff vehicle. I make my way out into the open as the officer steps out of the vehicle. They see me and pull their sidearm. I immediately put my hands in the air and stop as the officer shouts, "Identify yourself!"

I calmly say, "I am John Young, the owner of this property, and this is Dixie," as I point at my partner. The officer tells me to slowly get my ID out, and I reach into my pants pocket and pull out my wallet, keeping the other hand in plain sight. I have been on the other end of this moment too many times and know that until proven differently you can't let your guard down for even a moment. I have one bullet hole scar and one knife scar to prove it.

The officer I realize now is a woman and she says, "Toss your wallet over to me and put your hands on your head." I do as instructed, and she picks up my wallet and inspects the contents. She smiles and says, "Okay, John, you can put your hands down."

I smile back and tell her I had heard that the new sheriff here was a woman. She says, "Yep, that is me, Sheriff Cassie Quince. At

45

least I don't have to apologize to you for our introduction, John. You know the protocol. Welcome to my county, John. I have heard a lot about you. You are kind of a legend here in our little county."

I blush and try to deflect the compliment by saying, "I hear good things about you also sheriff."

She grins and says, "Please call me Cass, and thank you, John."

We stand for a moment in awkward silence, and I break it by saying, "I don't know what brought you out here, but I am glad to see you."

She replies, "We got an anonymous call that there was someone on the property. It was a burner cell, so we had no way to check the owner of the phone, and I figured I better come check this out myself so here I am."

I tell her we have a lot to talk about, and she says, "Let's have a seat on the swing, and you can tell me what's going on." I laugh and suggest that we don't set on the swing. We take a seat on the porch steps, and I give her the short version to bring her up to speed as quickly as I can.

She says, "Let's take a walk out to the barn and have a look in that cellar together." As we get up to go, Dixie lazily gets up from her nap on the porch, yawns, and gets in step with us.

As we walk, she asks me where I intend to spend the night, and I respond I had not really thought about that. She says, "Well, you are coming with me, and we will get you a hotel room for tonight. The owner of the Ford Dealership is my friend, so we will get a key made for your truck."

We make our way toward the barn, continuing our conversation about my day so far and getting acquainted with each other. The sheriff is intelligent and confident. Those two things, added to her simple beauty, make her very attractive.

Come on, John, let's get back on task here, I tell myself. It has been a long time since a woman had that effect on me. I must say it caught me off guard.

We enter the barn and turn on our flash lights as the daylight is really waning now. I fight the cellar door back open and drop it with a slam. I tell Dixie to stay, and she plops down at the top of the stairs. That darn dog amazes me.

Cass looks at me and says, "Your dog listens well."

I chuckle and say, "Not my dog."

She says, "Okay, tell me later."

We make our way down the steps and to the bottom, moving our lights across the room, and she immediately spots the area where the crates were sitting. She moves over to investigate and says, "I smell gun oil here."

I say to her, "Exactly what I surmised," and think to myself, *She is good.*

She says, "Let's get out of this cellar and go somewhere and talk this through." When we reach the top of the steps, Dixie meets us with a wagging tail, and Cass stops to pet her. She likes my dog. She does not look back at me and heads back to the house. Dixie and I follow her like two puppies. If I had a tail, it would be wagging just like Dixie's is now. I grin at Dixie, and she gives me a doggy grin back. Smart dog, smart dog.

When we get back to the house, Cass says, "Let's get the VIN number off of your dash so you can get a key made."

I ask her to wait a minute, and I go to my hiding place and get my duffel.

Cass says, "I see you are carrying, John. Do you still have a permit to carry that smoke wagon here in South Carolina?"

I laugh and say, "Yes ma'am." She gets better by the minute. That is a term from my favorite western Tombstone, and Curt Russel's character Wyatt Erp used that word. I repeat it in my head, *"Smoke wagon," where has she been all my life?*

I go and get my duffel and come back to find Cass and Dixie in the cruiser. Dixie is riding shotgun, and I complain about it to no avail. Cass says, "She told me you talk too much. She says you can ride in the back, John," and laughs as she says, "Okay, Dixie, in the back you go."

Dixie hops out and waits for me to open the door. I think the dog and the sheriff are both smarter than me.

I get in beside her, and she says, "Let's get to town and get you a room a shower some fresh clothes on, and a bite to eat. Then we are going to make a couple of visits to the town watering holes and talk to some locals. Are you in the mood to rattle a few cages John?"

I grin and tell her, "I was born for this."

She smiles a knowing smile and tells me, "So I have heard."

I don't rise to the bait, but I have a feeling that this lady is not afraid to do a little rattling herself. She continues to impress.

As we make our way back down the old driveway, she says, "It looks like there has been traffic here recently, and I noticed on the way in the gate latch was not rusted like I would have expected."

Did I mention she is impressive! I think to myself. I might be slipping, or was I just not expecting trouble? Either way I realize now that I was too involved with my memories of this place to have my eyes open to the signs around me.

The old driveway back out to the county road is rough and full of holes, but Cass handles the SUV like a pro. She is very comfortable in her skin and drives like she does everything else—with a quiet confidence. It is a half-hour drive back to town, and I say, "Tell me about yourself, Cass. How did you end up in this part of South Carolina and become the sheriff?"

Cass looks over at me and says, "It's a long boring story."

I say, "I have nothing but time. I am retired."

She smiles and says, "Okay, John, the short version will have to do for today."

I settle back into my seat and say, "We have twenty-five minutes or so until we get to town, you have the floor, sheriff."

She sighs and says, "Try to stay awake while I tell you, John. Compared to your life story, mine is pretty mundane."

I find myself quite intrigued by this woman, and I catch myself looking at her a little bit too intensely. I can tell that she notices it also, and I avert my gaze. Evidently it was the right moment to say something stupid, so I oblige and blurt out, "Are you married?"

She laughs and says, "Yes—to my work. How about you, John?"

I answer her, "No, divorced for many years because I was married to my work and just happened to live with my wife. Now back to your story please. Sorry to get us off track like that. I have found that asking seemingly random questions will more often than not give me an insight into the person I am questioning."

Cass laughs and says, "Bullcrap, you just wanted to know if I was single. And by the way I checked you for a ring already myself."

We share a smile, and she begins to tell me about her childhood. She says, "My father was a South Carolina state trooper, and I idolized him."

Every morning when he would walk into the kitchen with his uniform on, I thought that he was the most handsome man in the world.

He would kiss me on the cheek, and I would hug him, then he would kiss my mother and she would say to him, 'You be safe out there and come back home to me. I love you, Lieutenant.'

He would salute her and say, "Yes ma'am," and then he would take her face in his hands and kiss her forehead, step back put his hat on, smile, and say, "I love you both and I will see you tonight," and out the door he would go. It was the same every morning until one night he did not come home.

My mother and I were preparing to go ahead and eat supper because Dad was not home yet. Though he was home at a regular time each night, it was not unusual for him to be late once in a while. Tonight, it was already later than usual, and my normally calm mother was trying to put on her not-worried face but to no avail.

Finally, she said, "Cass, I am worried about your dad, he always calls if it is going to real late." Just then there was a knock on the door, Mom looked at me, and the tears welled up in her eyes. She said, "You wait right here, Cass, and let me see who is at the door."

I stayed put for all of one second and snuck over to the doorway of the kitchen that led down the hall to the front door. I peeked around the corner and saw two men talking softly to my mother. One was my dad's captain and another man I did not recognize. I ran down the hall, crying, "Mom, what's going on?"

My mother was crying and bent down and took me in her arms and said, "There has been an incident, and your father is in surgery right now. Go get your sweater and these men are going to take us to the hospital. Now you hurry, sweetie, your father needs us."

I ran to my room and got the sweater with ponies on it that Dad always said looked good on me. I was crying and shaking when I got back to Mom and the men. Mom held me a moment, composed herself, took my face in her hands, and said, "Your dad would want us to be strong. We are a trooper family."

I wiped my eyes and said, "Yes, ma'am," and out the door we went. My father died in surgery that day. He had been shot for no reason in a routine traffic stop by a guy out of his mind on meth. I was never quite the same after that. I grew up fast and really tough. I swore that I would continue the legacy of police work, and much to my mother's displeasure and constant pressure to pursue another line of work, here I am.

We had reached our destination and had been stopped for some time at this point and I look deep in her tear-filled eyes and I swear I fell in love with her that moment. I am overwhelmed with emotion and I want to hold her and tell her I knew how it felt to get your heart broken and to know exactly what you are called to do all at the same time. I realize that I was also crying, and it is Cass that holds me. We stay like that for a moment and then pull apart, both of us embarrassed and surprised.

I say, "Well, aren't we a pair? Let's get in here and get me a room before this turns into a Hallmark movie." We both laugh as the tension breaks and we make our way into the Wave Runner Hotel.

I see the desk clerk and think, *Oh crap*. Remember me telling you about the two bullies in my life and how that went for me? Here sits the one who cleaned my clock.

Cass looks at me. "Are you okay?"

I says, "Yeah, I am fine." I move up to the desk and say, "I need a room."

He looks me up and down and says, "John, is that you?"

I put on my best fake smile and say, "Yes, Jason, it is me."

CHAPTER 14

Home Sweet Home

It seems I am going from one awkward situation to another. I turn to Cass and say, "Jason and I know each other from our teenage days."

Jason looks at Cass and grins, and as soon as he starts talking, I know he has not changed. He says to Cass, "So Sheriff Quince, did Big John tell you how I kicked his butt on prom night our junior year?"

She answers, "No, he hasn't, Jason, but I have not told him yet how often I have to arrest you either. Perhaps we can share war stories another time, or better yet how about you give John here a rematch?"

I look at Cass incredulously, and she does not seem to notice me as Jason stutters "You mean right now?" and Cass says, "Yes, right now."

Jason stammers, "Well right now, I am on duty, and I can't leave my post."

Cass laughs and says, "This is the only good decision I have seen you make since I came to this county, Jason."

Jason looks at me and says, "Nice to see you, John. Would you be needing a room?"

It is all I can do to not laugh out loud as I answer, "Yes please."

Cass does not even flinch as she says, "I think it would be a nice gesture on your part, Jason, if you gave John here a complimentary room."

Poor Jason, he is trying to think of some way to save face, and I bail him out by saying, "My triple AAA discount would be enough."

He says, "How about half price?" and I say, "Great, lets end these negotiations."

"Done deal," Jason says, and I extend my hand. He takes it, and I hold on for just a moment and say, "It's okay, Jason, how about we let bygones be bygones?"

Jason is still kind of squirming, but he says, "Okay, John."

"Now I am going to my room and clean up quick while Cass here asks you some questions. I suggest that you answer her questions honestly and tell her anything you know. Let's have that room number and key please."

Jason hands me the key, and I see the room number is 112. I suddenly remember that Dixie is in the cruiser, and I ask Jason, "Do you allow pets?"

He says, "Not normally," and Cass says, "Let me take her home with me, John. I can feed her and pen her in the county kennel."

I say, "Are you sure?" and she looks at me like "Don't even start with me," and I say, "Okay."

As I walk away, I hear Cass say, "Okay, Jason, let's you and I have a little chat."

Duffel in hand, I make my way to my room open the door, step in, and shut it. I take a seat on the bed and think, *Finally for a moment, I can relax.* It has been one heck of a day so far.

I take my shoes off and lay back on the bed and close my eyes. For just a moment, I drift off, I think, but the phone next to the bed is ringing, and I reach over and pick it up. I say hello, and I hear a muffled voice say, "Don't speak and don't ask questions. Listen to me, John. Get out of here now. Leave town."

I hear a click, and the connection is broken. I run out of my room to the front desk and find Jason there, but Cass is not. I say to Jason, "Who the heck just called my room?"

He says, "They said they were family and asked to be transferred to your room."

I ask him, "where is Cass—I mean, the sheriff?"

Jason points at the window, and I see her on her radio by her SUV. I quickly go to and out the front door, and as I approach her, Cass looks at me with a surprised expression and says, "What are you doing out here? You are not even cleaned up yet."

I quickly tell her about the call, and she says, "Go get cleaned up, leave your door unlocked, and I will be in in a moment."

As I make my way back to the room, Jason starts to ask me a question, and I just hold my hand up and shake my head no.

My ex-wife used to say, "John, you can walk through a field of crap and come out on the other side smelling like a rose." So far today, I have walked through a field of crap and, well, I smell like crap. So much for her theory.

CHAPTER 15

Downtown, Everyone's Going There

I unpacked my few belongings and the dirty clothes I had removed at the plantation, then I undressed and hit the shower. I was just starting to relax as the steaming hot water washed over my tired, sore body when the bathroom door opened, and Cass said, "I am going to run home, clean up, and change clothes. I will meet you in a half hour at a little bar and grill down the street called the One-Eyed Fish. Go out the front door of the hotel and turn left."

I answered back "Okay, but don't you think it inappropriate to come into bathroom of a man you hardly know while he is showering?"

She laughed and said, "Well now, John, I thought we were closer than that," and off she went.

I chuckled to myself and thought, *That woman is one cool customer.*

I finished my shower, dried myself off with the cheap towel I found on the towel rack, and moved out into the room to put on some fresh clothes. I felt much better, and the thought of time with Cass had me wide awake. A little deodorant a shot of body spray, my best pair of worn-out jeans, a t-shirt that said, "Don't ask," and my favorite snake skin boots, and I was ready for the bar.

I ran my hands through my damp hair, looked in the mirror, and thought, *I used to be good-looking.*

I picked up all of my soiled clothes and walked up to the desk. Jason was sitting at the front desk, looking at a magazine when I walked up. He quickly hid the magazine, and I said, "What are you reading, Jason?"

He stuttered, "Ah, ah nothin'."

I laughed and said, "Is there a laundry service of some kind close here where I can get this stuff washed by morning?"

He gave me a blank look and said, "What?"

I said, "Do I need to say it slower?"

The light came on, and he said, "Oh yeah, our house cleaner will do it tonight for $10. Will be ready in the morning, and you can pick it up at the front desk at 7:00a.m."

I told him thanks, left the laundry on the counter, and headed for the front door. I could not help myself so I stopped, turned, and said, "I could see the magazine in the mirror behind you when I walked up, Jason."

He turned beet red kept his head down and said, "You can pay for your laundry in the morning."

I walked out the door and turned left. I could see the sign for the One-Eyed Fish about a block away so I made my way down the sidewalk with a spring in my step. I saw Cass standing by the front door, talking to someone, and as I approached, she turned grinned and waved and I waved back and smiled as I saw her expression change to one of panic. She screamed, "John, Look out!"

I saw the truck out of the corner of my eye and leaped to my left as it careened by me on the sidewalk. It took out a mail box and kept on going, leaving the bumper behind. I was a little scraped up but unhurt.

I sit up on the step of a little shop as Cass came running to me and helped me up. She said, "Are you okay, John?"

I answered, "Yes, I am fine," and she embraced me tightly and without reservation.

I returned the embrace and said, "In ancient Persian culture, if someone saved your life, you were indebted to them until you saved theirs. I owe you a life debt, Cass."

She laughed, released the embrace, and stepped back from me. She looked me straight in the eyes and said, "If I never collect, do you have to stay around?"

I said, "This place is pretty interesting. Maybe I should hang around just in case you need saving."

She said, "I dance to the beat of a different drum, John."

I grinned and said back to her, "The funny thing is, I hear the same one."

We both laugh out loud as we just shared the lyrics from a country song by Collin Raye. The song is titled "My Kind of Girl". I think to myself, *Be still, my heart, this is my kind of girl.*

I dust myself off and Cass loops her arm through mine. I say, "Madam, we have reservations at the One-Eyed Fish."

Cass asks, "Do you take all your lady friends there?"

I grin and say, "Only the ones I really like. The others I take to the Three-Legged Seagull."

Cass's laughter is like Christmas bells to my heart, and she shares it freely at that moment. She says, "You are one sweet talker, John Young." I am just the opposite, and she knows it, which makes her flirting that much attractive.

We have arrived at the "Fish," and I open the door for her and tell her, "Please lead the way, my lady, we are on your turf now."

She takes the lead and says, "I think tonight is a corner booth night, John."

I say, "Lead on," and she chooses a booth as far from the crowd as we can get. The crowd being thirteen people, a bartender, and a waitress. I peruse the room, noting the placement and body language of the clientele quickly.

When I look over at Cass, she says, "I watched you. What do you think?"

"Well, the guy at the bar by himself is a daily customer, not a drunk just nowhere to go. The couple in the corner is not married to each other. I mean, the woman at the bar is hoping a cute guy comes in, the couple in the other corner is married and on date night. The four guys over there are just drinking buddies, and the three girls over there are not interested in the four guys over there."

She laughs and says, "You are good, John Young."

I do a fake hat tip, and in my best John Wayne I say, "Thank you ma'am."

Cass makes me blush a little as she says, "The stories are wrong about you, John, you are kinda cute for a hard case."

I smile back and say, "And you are a spectacular woman, Cass Quince. If I walked in this bar and saw you, I would never even try to talk to you—heck, I couldn't pick you up in a bar if you came with a handle."

She looked at me for a second, and she laughed until tears came to her eyes. She said, "I have had men come on to me my whole life, and I have heard every kind of pick up line you can imagine, but John, that is the sweetest thing I have ever heard."

And then I really look at her, and it is like a frame from a Bokeh photograph. Everything around her is out of focus and all I see is her. Falling—I feel like I am falling.

Cass reaches across the table and takes my hand, pulls me back up. She looks in my eyes and says, "I know, John, me too."

CHAPTER 16

Made to Order

This time, there is no awkwardness between us as our eyes unlock, just a new feeling of "wow."

I say, "I am hungry. What is good here, Cass?"

She answers by saying, "I believe you like seafood, John."

I answer, "Yes. Growing up on the coast, I grew to love blue crab and oysters."

Cass smiles and says, "I read that in an interview you did after catching that serial killer about eight years ago. This place has great blue crab and some of the freshest oysters on the coast—also two of my favorites." Cass says, "Well then, may I order for us, sir?"

I answer her, "Yes, you may, madam."

"And what would you like to drink, John?"

I answer her, "Water with lemon," and she raises her eyebrows and says, "Really?"

I answer her, "Yes. I quit drinking about five years ago, Cass."

Cass grins and says, "I had heard you were a bit of a drinker."

I chuckle and say, "Yeah, a bit of a drinker."

She says, "Okay, topic for a different time," as the waitress arrives. Cass places our order and leans forward and says, "I think that there is a place on the outside edge of town we should go to after we eat. My CI is a frequent flyer at that establishment, and I have not rousted him for a while."

Our waitress arrives with our two waters, lemon on the side, and we both squeeze a lemon wedge into our waters and raise our glasses to each other.

"You or me?" she asks.

I say, "I will do the honors. To a new partnership, to a case to solve, to the future, to surprise encounters, and to us, my lady, I salute you."

She laughed, we sipped, and we slipped into conversation about the events of the day at the plantation. Our oysters arrived, and she was right—they were amazing.

Conversation took a break as we focused on the task of slurping down the oysters. We took time to smile at each other and say things like "Man, these are good," and "These are amazing"—you know, stuff like that. It was comfortable and fun, but the underlying sensual tension was the best part of the appetizer.

Our crab came with melted butter, rosemary garlic potato wedges, and a sweet dinner roll. The conversation was free and easy throughout the meal, and the evening was going along so smoothly when Cass got a call on her cellphone.

I could see by the look on her face that it was not good news. I sat quietly and listened to one side of the conversation as I heard the "Yes, Bill, I am at the Fish. Okay I know the place. Who found him? Yeah, has anyone moved the body? Okay, don't let anyone near the scene. Yes, rope it off. We will be there in twenty minutes."

Cass disconnects, looks at me, and says, "They found a body out along the beach, south of your property." Cass stands up and flags our waitress down and says, "Put this on a tab. I will be back in tomorrow to pay. We need to leave now."

The waitress asks, "Is everything okay?" and Cass says, "Oh yeah, a little problem on the beach, Cheryl." Cheryl keeps glancing at me as they talk so Cass says, "Cheryl, this is Sheriff John Young from Raleigh North Carolina. He grew up here and is visiting."

Cheryl says, "Nice to meet you, Sheriff," and I tell her, "Thank you but the pleasure is all mine."

Cass says, "We need to get going," so we quickly make our exit. As we leave, Cheryl says, "Come back again, sheriff," and Cass laughs and says, "I think she was talking to you, John."

I laugh and say, "Everwhat," and Cass stops looks at me and says, "You are an enigma, John Young."

I answer, "Thank you," and Cass says, "That wasn't really a compliment."

I chuckle, and we head for the cruiser. When we reach the cruiser, I ask, "Can I drive?" and she ignores me and gets in the driver's seat. As I buckle up, she says, "You are retired. I drive."

She waits until we hit the edge of town before she flips on the flashers, and off we go. She radios Bill, the deputy who called it in, and lets him know we are on the way. She glances over at me and says, "What I have been thinking? There is a good chance this is the victim from the shot you heard, John."

I say, "Yes, quite probably it is."

We both go silent as we consider the situation. Silence may not be golden, but it is almost always the sound you don't hear before a bang.

CHAPTER 17

Beaches

When we arrive at the beach area, we park at the top of the hill along the rocks that look out over the ocean. There is an area along the roadside where there is room to park about four or five cars. Cass grabs two flashlights and hands me one. We turn them on and shine them out in front of us to light the path.

From where we are standing, we can see the lighted area on the beach where the body is. The path down to the beach is a combination of sand and crushed rocks, and Cass says to me, "You're gonna wish you did not have those boots on, John."

As we make our way down the hill, it is clear that she is right. The stones are loose and slippery, and footing is bad, but there is no way in heck that I am going to fall. Cass beats me down the hill by quite a distance stops and turns and hollers up at me, "Are you coming John, or did you stop to rest?"

I yell back, "Go ahead, I am collecting evidence!"

She yells back and laughs. "Everwhat."

I see her flashlight move down the beach, and I direct mine back to the path. As I start to move, I notice a footprint that is off of the stones and in the mud along the path going up the hill. It is a boot print—a boot print like the ones at the plantation.

I yell at Cass and she stops turns toward me and I yell, "Send a patrolman up here to rope off an area!" Before she can ask, I yell, "I will explain when I get down to you!" She turns and moves toward the lighted area.

When the officer gets to me, I tell him, "Be sure and get pictures of the print and a casting."

He says quite seriously, "Who are you?"

I am a little embarrassed as I say, "Retired Sheriff John Young."

He smiles and says, "She told me to say that."

I say, "You know what, that is not a surprise."

The officer says, "I will take care of this, sir. She is waiting on you at the beach."

I thank him and head down the hill. I am chuckling to myself as I work my way down the hill. I can see the lighted area just a little way up the beach, and Cass is talking to a man I assume is the coroner as they examine the body. I walk up to Cass, and she says, "Now don't you mess up my crime scene."

I say, "Yes, ma'am."

We slip back into serious mode as Cass introduces me to the coroner. Cass says to me, "This is our county coroner and the owner of the local Funeral Home and Crematorium," but before she can say his name, he turns to acknowledge me, and I recognize him right away. He is Mark Hampton, the son of the Funeral Home director who took care of my father when he passed. I have not seen Mark for at least thirty-six years.

Cass sees that we obviously know each other and asks, "Do I want to know how you two know each other?"

I say, "I will tell you later, but I can tell you he has never punched me, and I have never punched him."

Cass says, "Finally, someone you have not punched. Let's get to work here."

As we examine the body, Mark says, "It looks like he was dumped here." There are tire tracks from an ATV that came from the west. You can see that the waves have washed most of the tracks away. It appears that the victim has a bullet wound in the thigh area, and it looks like the bullet must have nicked the femoral artery because the victim bled out. I am guessing that wound was not meant to be fatal. The ATV then went on down the beach, and we lose the tracks in the wash. The victim has no ID on him. He is a white male approximately thirty-five to forty years old.

Cass says Mark has examined the body and is ready to have it taken back to the morgue. One deputy helps Mark bag the body, and Cass says to me, "Let's you and I walk the beach area and talk, John."

Cass and I slowly move along the beach our flashlights, probing the darkness as the waves slap the sand. Cass asks me what I found up on the footpath so I tell her about the boot print. It seems to me that the print was left by someone standing, looking down at the beach. If someone was observing the body dump, why did they not report it? The obvious answer is that they are guilty of something also. We discuss the events at the plantation, the gunshot, the blood, and the ATV.

The gunshot, the blood and the ATV—sounds like the name of a country song. The irony is not lost on us as we talk about the obvious link.

We decide to go back to the plantation in the morning for a blood sample to see if it matches the body. Cass and I continue along the beach in silence flashlights, searching the sand for clues, and in the darkness, we brush up against one another. I feel the electricity of her touch and stop in my tracks as the goose bumps jump up on my arm.

Cass asks, "Are you cold, John?" and shines her flashlight on me.

I say, "No, but I probably should have brought a jacket."

She says, "Maybe one of the officers has something with them that would fit you, and what does that mean on your t-shirt anyway?"

I laugh and ask her, "What does my shirt say?"

Cass laughs and says, "It says don't ask."

I try my best to be serious and say, "Is there some part of that that is not clear to you?"

Cass says, "Well, John, I am a woman and a cop. You do the math."

I tell her, "It is the title of the book written about one of my arrests."

She says, "Oh yes, the serial killer you took down."

I bashfully answer, "Yeah, something like that."

Cass says, "Really, John, I have read the book. It is very good, and I know it made the Times' Best Seller list."

I answer, "Yes, it was, and it allowed me to retire while I was still young and not dead."

Cass asks, "How old are you, John?"

I say, "It is not polite to ask a man his age."

Cass replies, "It is if you want to know how old he is."

I laugh and tell her, "Fifty-four."

She says, "I guess that will do."

I think about responding, but I hold my tongue. I am considering how I am going to ask Cass her age when she stops, does not look back, and says, "Forty-seven," then starts walking again. Can she read my mind?

We wrap up our search of the beach area, and Cass says, "Let's head back up to the vehicle, John." We make our way back up the path and stop to look at the footprint area. We discuss the similarities of this print and what I remember of the print at the plantation. They are definitely the same kind of boot.

I look at Cass, and with my most serious face, I say, "The game is afoot."

Cass looks at me and says, "You are such a nerd. But a darn good-looking one."

I smile, and I have something to say back, but I hold my words. Sometimes not speaking is, well, a good way to be quiet.

CHAPTER 18

Grave Matters

Cass and I make our way back to the SUV, and as I move around to her side to open the door for her, she politely steps back and allows me the honor. As she steps in, she proclaims, chivalry is not dead," and I say, "Which is more than we can say for the guy on the beach."

I take my place in the passenger seat, and we both buckle up. Cass looks over at me and says, "Tell me about you and Mark, John."

I say, "There is not much to tell Cass," and she says, "I saw the faraway look in your eyes, John."

I am quiet as my mind takes a road trip. In my memory, I arrive at the Hampton Funeral Home the Christmas Day my dad died.

Cass breaks the silence when she asks me, "Where are you, John?"

I stay at the funeral home in my mind but answer her question in the now. "I am at the Hampton Funeral Home the day my father died."

Cass says nothing, but she does not start the truck.

I was thirteen and standing beside my grandpa and grandma in the parlor of the funeral home. Shock and grief were my comrades as I stood there. Mark's father, Paul, entered, and the conversation about arrangements began. The whole conversation seemed surreal, and I was a bystander as they talked.

Out of the corner of my eye, I saw a boy about my age watching us from the other room. I moved away from the adults, and the boy in the other room waved for me to come to him. I didn't say anything but slipped away from the adults, and no one seemed to notice as I left.

I walked up to him, and he said, "Let's get out of here."

I followed him outside, and he headed toward the creek. I silently walked a few steps behind until we reached the creek. We stopped under a giant willow, and he turned to me and said, "First time in a funeral home?"

I said, "Yes, pretty obvious, huh?"

He said, "Yeah, but don't feel bad most people are not comfortable when they come here. I have spent my whole life here, so I don't see it the same as you. Perception is everything." He stopped, offered his hand and said, "My name is Mark."

I said, "And mine is John."

We shook hands and sat down on a log by the creek. There were stones by the log, and we both bent and picked up a handful and started tossing them in the water as boys will do when they are bored or nervous. Finally, I broke the silence by doing what I have always done well: I asked a stupid question. "Have you seen a lot of dead bodies?"

Mark looked at me grins and said, "Yeah, and a lot of zombies too."

I looked at him, and he had the most serious look on his face, but it turned to a Cheshire grin rather quickly. I asked, "Is it true you have to cut their heads off?" and he said, "Yes, but you can also dispatch them by shooting them in the head or stabbing them in the head."

I laughed for the first time all day and asked, "How many have you dispatched so far?"

He said, "So far about fifty. We have a lot of them in this area, John."

I said, "Perhaps I can hunt them with you someday, Mark." Little did I know that one day I would hunt something far worse. Mark and I go back to throwing stones, but now the quiet is comfortable.

Mark started to talk again, and I could tell he had something important to say to me. Mark looked at me and said, "How bad does it hurt?"

I asked him, "How bad does what hurt?"

He said to me, "You know darn well what I mean."

I said, "Yeah I know. It hurts real bad, the kind of bad that you think you can't stand any longer, but it gets worse."

Mark said to me, "My dad sees it all the time, and he talks to me about it when we fish together. Dad said that people too often allow the death of a loved one to define them and their existence. He compared it to a falling star. He said that when people see a star falling, they are amazed at the significance and the beauty of it.

"Dad says, 'Why are we not amazed that millions of them stay in the sky every day? Stars are not defined by falling, and life is not defined by dying, it is defined by living. If we celebrate the time our loved ones were shining, it makes the grief of the falling easier to bare.'"

I cried and I sobbed and the pain washed over me like a giant wave, but like any wave, it receded, and I was left on the beach soaked to the bone, but the sun started to come out and the pain started to ease and I knew I would be fine and I knew that dad was fine too.

I looked over at Mark, and he had tears in his eyes as he tells me his mother is dying of cancer. He said to me, "We don't know each other very well, but I need you to make me a promise, John." I tell him I will. He said, "When my mom goes, I need you to tell me the same story." I promised him, and we shook hands.

From that day on until our senior year, Mark and I were very close. His mom fought the good fight until that senior year. When she passed away, I took Mark to the log by the creek told him the story, but it did not have the same effect on him it had on me. Mark told me thanks for keeping my promise, did not shed a tear, and got up from the log by the creek and never spoke to me again.

"Such is life. Stars fall, stars stay in the sky. People live, and people die. We allow events to define us or we choose what defines us. Life is a lesson, Cass. Today was the first time Mark has spoken to me since his mother passed."

Cass has tears in her eyes and puts her hand on mine. She looks deep in my eyes and says, "Welcome home, John."

CHAPTER 19

I Love the Night Life

Cass releases my hand wipes her eyes and says, "Tell me a funny story, John."

I say, "Okay, Cass."

When I was a rookie cop, I was assigned to a precinct in the heart of Raleigh, and there was a really pretty girl named Charlene in the coffee shop across the street where all the officers got coffee. Most of them just because she was so pretty. They told me that she was deaf but was an incredible lip reader so when you ordered, it was important to look right in her eyes and to talk very deliberately, but if you turned away, she would not be able to understand what you said.

So each day, I would go in and order my plain black coffee, and I would enunciate all my words slowly and with exaggerated expressions. I would turn and tell my partner that she was the finest woman I had ever seen and told him I was going to take signing classes, so I could talk to her better. I would say each day to my partner as we walked out that I wanted to ask her out, but I was afraid she would not want to go out with me.

After about a week one day, I walked up to her and ordered my coffee, paid for it and turned to go and heard these words, "John, I would love to go out with you."

I turned to see who said it, and Charlene was smiling broadly as she said, 'I guess I owe you an apology, John, your partner and his buddies set you up."

I turned back to look at the other officers in the shop, and they were all laughing and exchanging money as they had bet on whether she would go out with me. I turned back to Charlene, and she said, "I get off at seven, John." I asked if I may pick her up after, and she said, "Yes, you may, sir."

I turned back to my partner and he said, "I lost 20 bucks on you, John. She never goes out with cops." I married her a year later.

Cass says, "Good story but not as funny as I was hoping for. You need to work on your delivery, John.

I tell her, "Thank you for your critique of my storytelling abilities, my lady, but that is why I had an editor for my book."

She laughs and says, "Okay, big man, time to rattle them cages."

I say, "Let's go, sheriff."

Cass starts the SUV, and we head back up the coast toward town. I ask her where we are going, and she says to a little bar on the outskirts of town called the Park Station. I ask her why the name and she says, "Because it is stationed on the edge of the state park."

I think to myself, *Don't say a thing, John.* We take off for the bar, and the stones fly as Cass hits the gas. The ride to the bar is uneventful, and we arrive there in about fifteen minutes.

Cass shuts off the truck and tells me to play along. She says, "My CI's name is Cleland Inman."

I say, "Seriously?"

"Seriously. All CIs are named after him," she says in a most serious of tones.

I say, "Mm, I always thought that meant confidential informant."

She says, "No, it means Cleland Inman."

I say, "I am shocked."

She says, "You don't know much for a big city cop."

I laugh and say, "are we going to talk all night or are we going to go rattling?"

Cass says, "Let's shake, rattle, and roll, big man."

We exit the vehicle, and Cass leads the way. When we enter the bar, it is noisy, and you can see it is a rough crowd. Cass stops after the door goes shut and looks around slowly.

As we stand there, I see the crowd slowly become aware of our presence, and the noise level goes down a few decibels. Cass walks up to the bar and asks the bartender if Cleland is here. He points to the back room, and we head back there, all eyes on us as we move through the room.

About halfway back, a big biker looking guy steps in front of me and puts his hand on my shoulder and asks what I am doing in his bar.

I politely tell him that I am with the sheriff, and if he does not remove his hand, I will break it.

He grins his four-toothed grin and takes a swing with his other hand. I duck, feint to my left, and catch him with a solid right cross on the left cheek bone and down he goes. I step on his hand and stomp my boot down hard. He hollers in pain, and I say, "I warned you."

Cass says, "Was that really necessary?" and I say, "Yeah."

She says, "Okay."

We make our way to the back room through a now much quieter bar. She spots Cleland, and he is looking at us like he wants to be someplace else right now. Cass walks up and says, "We need to talk to you, Cleland."

He asks Cass, "Who is the cowboy?"

Cass says quite loudly to the whole room, "This is my new friend, Sheriff John Young. Perhaps some of you have heard of John."

I look around the room and access the threat level of each patron and see no imminent danger. Cass tells Cleland we need to go outside and talk. He starts to protest, and I whisper to him that his cooperation is not optional.

He seems to understand the nuance of the moment and says, "Let's go out the back door."

We follow close behind him, and as he exits the back door, he slams it in our face and takes off running. Cass gets out the door in front of me and takes off after him. I follow her out the door, and they are already a long way in front of me.

I look at the terrain quickly and make a decision to cut the way there is no street lights. I run diagonal to the path they are headed on and cut through an alley. When I come out on the other side, I hear Cass shout at Cleland to stop or she is going to shoot him.

I think to myself, *He had better stop*. I take off again through another alley, and as I come out the other side, I see Cass lunge and tackle Cleland hard into a group of trash cans.

When I reach them, she has him on his belly and is handcuffing him. She is not even breathing hard, and I am out of breath. She does not have much sympathy for Cleland as she drags him to his feet the whole time whining that she is hurting him.

She says, "Shut up, Cleland! Why did you run?"

He says, "Because I didn't think you could catch me."

I stop grinning when Cass looks at me and says, "Where were you?"

I say, "I would have got him if you didn't. I just wanted you to get the collar."

Cass says, "Aren't you the gentleman?"

I say, "Why yes, I am, but I would have shot him."

Cleland starts to protest and Cass says, "If you want to be tased, keep yapping." He gets quiet fast, and Cass says to him, "Now get your breath, and then I have some questions for you."

Everyone is calm now, and cooler heads are prevailing as Cass asks Cleland, "Now, again, why did you run?"

He says to her, "There are some bad men in town, and crossing them is a good way to get dead. By running, I removed suspicion from myself. Plus, I really didn't think you could catch me."

Cass says, "I heard you the first time. So what is going on here and who are these men?"

Cleland answers, "I have not seen them, I just know the talk on the street is they are bad dudes. There is word of a gun shipment that went south on them, and someone local is involved."

Cass says, "What else?" and Cleland says, "That is all I know."

Cass says, "If I find out you are lying to me, I will put the word out that you are a snitch."

Cleland says, "No way I lie to you, sheriff."

Cass says, "Okay, I am going to take you in, and you can spend the night in my jail. We will let you out in the morning."

Cleland starts to protest again, and Cass gets out her taser. He says, "Okay, no problem."

Cass calls for a cruiser to meet us at the bar, and we walk him back. The cruiser arrives and Cass gives them their instructions and off goes Cleland with most of the bar outside watching. Cass yells at the crowd, "Show's over!" and they make their way back into the bar.

Cass and I get back in the SUV, and I say, "You sure know how to show a guy a good time."

She laughs and says, "The night is young."

Once again, I think to myself, *Don't say anything*. But darn it, that was funny. The night is "Young."

I ask, "Where to next?" and Cass says, "I think we both need to get some sleep and start again in the morning."

I agree, and she heads us back to my hotel. When we reach the Wave Runner, Cass stops by the front door, and I say to her, "Thank you for a wonderful night."

She laughs and says, "Are you going to punch someone every time we go out?"

I laugh and say, "Probably," and she says, "Okay. Good night, John, I will pick you up at 7:00a.m."

I stand and watch as she pulls away, and I say to no one in particular, "What a woman."

I fish my room key out of my pocket and head to my room. I unlock and carefully open the door to my room. Everything seems to be in place and ok. I set the alarm, turn the TV on, and hit the bed. I try to process the day, but all I can think about is Cass. Sleep comes to me quickly, and I dream the dreams of a man falling in love.

CHAPTER 20

Morning Is Broken

Somewhere in the night, my dream goes to a memory I don't have. I dream of my mother.

My mother died in childbirth—mine. All I have is a pair of paintings she did, pictures of her, and the stories my father and grandparents told me growing up. My mother loved to paint, and she loved the plantation, so her paintings were of the property surrounding the old house. I know the house was not always old, but to me it is always "the old house." My favorite painting is of the sun setting behind the pond, and there is a deer drinking from the pond in the last light of the day. It hangs on the wall of my home in Raleigh above my fireplace.

In my dream, I am looking at the painting, and as I look at it, I can see my mom setting at her easel on the other side of the pond, painting the scene in front of her. I can see the look in her eyes as she studies the scene and the light that shimmers in them as she transfers the scene to the canvas. She is beautiful, and it is as though she is sitting in a lighted area as everything around her grows darker.

As I watch her, I realize that the light is emanating from her, not from around her. She looks up at me and smiles and says, "Do you like the painting, John?"

I say, "Yes, I love it, Mom. I have it above my fireplace."

She smiles again and says, "Yes, I know." And she is gone.

I look all around for her, but she is nowhere to be found. I yell out, "Mom, where are you?"

I turn, and there stands my father. He says, "John, calm mind. Be still. All storms must pass." I close my eyes and take a deep breath. With my eyes still shut, I hear my father say, "John, you know where we are. We are waiting on you to join us but not yet."

In my dream, I see a single pane of a four-pane glass window. I look at it closely and I see my face in it and then it explodes, shards of glass flying everywhere. I awaken, drenched in sweat.

As I lay there, I feel a calm come over me. I know why I came, now I know why I am here.

My encounter with Mark opened a wound in me that had scabbed over but had never healed. I remembered something that my dad told me that mom said to him as she was leaving us. She said, "The day comes when we all must die, be sure to live all the rest of them."

CHAPTER 21

New Days

I lay in the bed, shaking the dream cobwebs out of my head, and a calmness comes over me. A peace that I have not felt, well, ever. I close my eyes, and I picture my mother by the pond. I smile in my heart and consider my life up to this moment. A snapshot of it, if you will, all leading up to "now." It would appear that I am being cleansed and renewed. A new day has dawned.

I have a vitality and a bounce in my step as I get out of the cheap hotel bed. The floor is cold on my bare feet, and the air in the room has a nice chill that that sends me to the bathroom for a hot shower. I let the water get good and hot, and the bathroom starts to steam up as I undress and get in the shower. I adjust the water temperature to as hot as I can stand it and turn my face up into the stream.

As I stand there, I can feel years of pain and anger wash off of me, and it is as if weight is being removed from me and washed down the drain. I am thankful for this refreshing of my soul, and I offer up a prayer of thanks. I shut the water off, get out of the shower, dry off, and wrap a towel around me.

As I open the bathroom door to step out, my room door opens and in walks Cass. I ask her, "Don't you knock?" and she responds, "Police business."

I say, "Don't you need a warrant?" and she says, "Probable cause."

I see she has a bag in her hand, and she sets it on the bed and says, "Your clothes, John."

I say, "Thank you, ma'am," and Cass says, "You get dressed, I have something else for you. I will be back in a moment."

I get myself dressed, and the door opens and in bursts Dixie! She runs to me, and to my surprise, she sits right in front of me, eyes sparkling and tongue hanging out. I say, "Good girl," and tell her to come over here, and she pushes up against me as I pet her.

Cass says, "So how did you two meet?"

I laugh and tell her the short version including the background of my original Dixie. Cass has a faraway look in her eyes as I finish the story, and I want to ask, but she senses it and says, "Okay, let's get the move on, John."

She has a box she has been holding since she came in, and she hands it to me and says, "I brought these for you, John."

I open the box, and it is a pair of lightweight patrol boots. I thank her and try them on. They are perfect and feel great on my feet. I ask her, "How did you know my size?"

She says, "You are not the only cop here, you know."

I laugh and say, "No, you are. I am retired."

Cass says to me, "Let me take a look at you, John. Something is different about you." I smile broadly, and she says, "Exactly, the sadness that I saw in your eyes when we met is gone. What's going on with you, cowboy?"

I laugh and say, "I met a girl."

She looks at Dixie and says, "You lucky dog." She turns her back and says, "Let's go eat."

She turns back and grins at me, and I say, "What's going on with you and that smart-aleck grin?"

She says, "I met a guy, and who is this Alec you speak of?" Man, this woman gets me. Rephrase that—has me.

I grab my few belongings, and I say goodbye to the Wave Runner Motel. I walk out the door and see my two girls sitting in the SUV—this time Dixie is in the back. I open the passenger door, take my place beside Cass, and she hands me a pair of sunglasses. I put them on, pull my seatbelt on, and snap myself in, pull the door shut and lean back in my seat. I feel good.

Cass looks over at me, laughs, and says, "If you were any cooler, I would have to turn on the heater."

I do something completely out of character for me. I give her a hearty laugh and say, "I have been working on this look for years, and it looks like all that was missing was you."

Cass laughs and says, "Let's go, player," and off we go.

CHAPTER 22

Don't Clam Up on Me

I look in the back seat, and Dixie has settled in and is looking out the window as we pull away from the motel. I turn to Cass and ask her where we are going to eat.

She grins and says, "Saul's Clam Castle."

I laugh and say, "A little early for clam, isn't it?"

"They have all kinds of food, but they are known for their clams." Cass says, "They have a great breakfast skillet named 'the bait bucket.'"

I say, "Now that sounds appetizing," and Dixie gives a woof of approval. I look at Cass and say, "Don't' pay any attention to her, she eats dog food."

Cass laughs and says, "Now remember and try not to punch anyone."

I grin back at her and say, "No promises." I am glad I have the glasses on, so she can't see the way I am looking at her.

I put my attention back to the road ahead, and we travel for a few miles in silence—a comfortable silence. Up ahead, I see the sign for Saul's, and Cass says, "I hope you are as hungry as I am."

I say, "I am famished," and Dixie gives another woof.

Cass speaks up and says, "Dixie, I fed you before we left. You have to wait in the SUV."

Dixie lays down in the backseat as Cass pulls into the diner, and I am amazed at the rapport between the two of them. I laugh as I tell Dixie, "The difference between you two is her bite is probably worse than your bark."

Cass quickly responds, "And don't you forget it."

I say, "Let's eat, my lady, and may I get your door?"

Cass says, "You, sir, are a gentleman, but I can't let you open my door today. I am the sheriff here."

I agree with her and say, "Perhaps another time."

She says, "Most definitely another time, sir."

We both laugh as we exit the SUV and head for the entrance to Saul's. As we enter the diner, I do my usual survey of the room, and out of the corner of my eye, I see Cass doing the same thing. Both of us satisfied with our surveys, we look at each other and say "table" at the same time.

We laugh and walk to the corner of the room by instinct, so we can watch the door, and our backs are protected. There is an easiness about our interaction today, and I like it.

Cass looks at me and says, "Okay, cowboy, what's going on with that stupid grin that seems to be stuck on your face?"

I give her a big smile and say, "You mean this one?" and she says, "No, not the dork smile. The grin that is on your face now." I look at her, and she says, "John, let's have it."

I look at her, and she puts me at ease simply by saying, "Don't clam up on me now," and I laugh until tears are rolling down my cheeks. To my surprise, I find myself recounting the dream to her and I am not embarrassed or hesitant.

When I finish, Cass does that thing again where she takes my hand, and this time I embrace hers also. Cass gives me a look that melts my heart and says, "John, I am glad you are here," and I respond, "So am I, Cass."

We both see the waitress come out of the back and quickly release our hands. The waitress comes over and says, "Hello, sheriff."

Cass smiles and says, "Good morning, Lisa, how are the girls?"

Lisa says, "They are fine, and little Janey still is saying she wants to be a cop."

Cass laughs as she says, "Let's see if I remember correctly. Janey is four."

Lisa says, "You remember right, sheriff."

Cass says, "You tell her to come see me in fourteen years, and we will talk."

Lisa says, "You got it, sheriff. How about a couple of cups of coffee for you and the gentleman?"

Cass laughs and says, "This is no gentleman, Lisa, this is Sheriff John Young."

I stand, tip my hat, and say, "Retired Sheriff John Young. Nice to meet you, Lisa."

Lisa says to Cass, "Seems like a gentleman to me, sheriff."

Cass says, "Don't fall for his big-city charm, Lisa."

I smile, sit back down, and say, "Okay, Lisa, tell me about the bait bucket."

Lisa says, "It is our signature breakfast, John, and if you are a big breakfast eater, I suggest you give it a try."

I say, "Tell me what's in the bait bucket."

She says, "Three homemade buttermilk biscuits, our sausage gravy made with a spicy sausage packed right here along the coast by a local farm, four slices of thick brown sugar bacon from the same farm, three eggs cooked to order topped with shredded provolone and cheddar cheese, and a sprinkling of fresh parsley all on a bed of our crispy hash browns."

I say, "Hook me up."

Lisa looks at Cass and says, "How about you, sheriff?"

Cass says, "I may have to run a perp down today, and it looks like Sheriff Young won't be able to catch anyone, so French toast and sausage for me, Lisa."

Lisa says, "I will put your order in and bring you your coffee and waters right away."

Off Lisa goes, and Cass and I turn our attention back to each other. Cass says, "Let's talk about Joseph."

I say, "What do you know about him?"

Cass says, "Well, he lives in a small house out near the plantation property and he seldom comes in to town and his house is a long way off of the main road, so you can't even see it from the highway."

I tell her that is the property that my grandparents gave to his family years ago. Cass asks me to explain a comment that I made to her about Joseph and I having some issues in our youth when I was giving her the initial rundown on my day up to when she arrived at the plantation.

I tell her the story of Dixie and my repeated run-ins with Joseph. I tell her that there was a hurt in Joseph that drove his anger, and I never knew what it was until much later in life. Cass asks me if I want to share it with her, and I close my eyes and fall silent for a moment as the memory fills my mind.

Lisa breaks the silence of the moment by arriving with our food, and I tell Cass, "Let's eat and then I will tell you a tale of bad blood and forbidden love."

Cass says, "Sounds like a romance novel title."

I say, "I guess you could say that," and take a bite of my bait bucket. Lisa has refilled our coffee cups and is waiting for my approval of the food. I tell her, "It is wonderful," and she smiles and leaves us to eat our breakfast. Cass and I eat in silence, but once again, it is a comfortable silence. It is nice being with her, and it is nice not being alone.

CHAPTER 23

Blood and Lies

After we finish our meal, Cass says, "There is a nice deck on the back here. How about we get our cups refilled and go out there and you can tell me this tale of bad blood and forbidden love?"

I agree, and Lisa appears with a pot of coffee, tops us off, and Cass lays a twenty down and tells Lisa keep the change and that we are going out back to finish our coffee. Lisa thanks Cass and says, "Nice to meet you, John."

I return the nice to meet you, and Cass leads the way out to the deck. She is right—it is beautiful out here, and we take seats across from each other. I sit down and close my eyes again as I let the memory fill my mind. Cass is silent as I clear my mind of the present and the moment in time becomes very real again.

I still have my eyes closed as I start the story:

My grandma had been gone for a few years, and Grandpa was on his deathbed when I arrived at the plantation. It was raining so hard that you might think the sky was falling. The caregiver that my brother and I had hired met me at the front door as I ran it from my truck. The old coat rack was there and as menacing as ever. The caregiver's name was Thomas. His family has been friends with ours for many years. Grandpa would have nothing to do with a woman taking care of him if it wasn't Grandma, so he had agreed to let Thomas stay at the house with him. Thomas was a good-sized man and able to handle grandpa without any trouble at all.

Thomas took my jacket and asked me about my trip in from Raleigh. I told him it was uneventful and asked about Grandpa. Thomas said he was slipping fast and did not expect him to last much longer and that he had been asking about me.

I went to his room and tapped on the door. I opened it slowly and saw that his eyes were closed so I entered quietly and took the chair beside his bed and sat down to wait on Grandpa to awaken. I had set there for just a moment when I heard his scratchy old voice say, "I am awake, boy. It's about time you got here."

I said, "Hi gramps, how are you doing?"

Grandpa said, "I told you not to call me gramps, and other than the fact that I am going to die any minute, I am fine."

I said, "Sorry, sir."

Grandpa cackled at me and said, "Don't get all worked up, John, I have lived long enough. There are some things I need to tell you before I die, so you be quiet and listen."

I said once again, "Yes sir."

I leaned back in the chair, and Grandpa said, "Do you remember my brother Gary, John?"

I said, "Faintly, Grandpa. I was pretty young, but didn't he disappear?"

Grandpa said, "Yes and no."

I said, "What does that mean, sir?"

Grandpa said, "I know where he is."

I said, "Where?"

Grandpa closed his eyes, exhaled a raspy breath. I leaned forward in my chair, and his next words stunned me. "He is buried in the swamp behind the pond, John."

Gary was a first mate in the Merchant Marine and was gone most of the time at sea, so we seldom saw him, but when he was home, he would stay at the plantation. I asked, "What do you mean he is buried in the swamp?"

He said, "One summer, when he was on shore leave for a couple weeks and staying with us, he struck up a friendship with Esther."

I said, "Jerry's Esther?"

He said, "Yes, Jerry's Esther. One afternoon when we got in from the fields, Jerry dropped me off and headed home for the evening. About a half hour later, I heard his truck pull up outside the house and the door slam. I got to the front door just as he hit the steps. Jerry had a wild look in his eyes and he said, 'I need you to get in the truck and come with me right now.'"

I hopped in and smelled gun powder and saw a handgun laying on the seat beside him.

I said, "What's going on, Jerry?"

He said, "I didn't mean to shoot him."

I said, "Stop the truck now, Jerry," but he just kept driving. I said, "Who did you shoot?"

He hit the brakes, slid to a stop, looked at me, and said, "Your brother." Before I could say anything, he said, "I walked into my house, and he was in bed with my wife. I walked over to the dresser and took my handgun out of the drawer, and I shot him."

I said, "How could you just shoot him like that? Esther is just as much to blame."

He said, "When I confronted him, he laughed at me and said that if I was taking care of my wife, this would not have happened, and I said then this would not have happened either and I shot him right between the eyes." He put the truck back in gear and took off.

"John, I was in shock. My brother was dead, Jerry was a murderer, and Esther was an adulterer."

Jerry looked straight ahead and said, "I know everything about the smuggling you and Gary were doing."

I asked, "So what are you saying, Jerry?"

He said, "I am saying help me, or I tell the authorities everything, and your family goes down."

I didn't respond, and we pulled up to his house. The front door was open, and we walked in together and found Esther at the kitchen table, covered in Gary's blood. She was obviously in shock, and I didn't even try to talk to her. We went into the bedroom, and Gary was laying across the end of the bed with most of his forehead gone.

"It was a heck of a mess, John."

Jerry and I wrapped Gary in the sheet off of the bed, and as we carried him through the house on our way out to the truck, Jerry told Esther to get the bedroom and herself cleaned up before he got back. We went out and put him in the bed of the truck. Jerry went to the shed and got two shovels and threw them in the back of the truck. We still had not spoken yet, and Jerry got on the old logging road that goes out to the swamp.

He followed the old road until it ends, and we got out of the truck. We went around our opposite sides of the truck and met by the tailgate. He stopped and looked at me, and I hit him with a solid right cross. He went down hard and lay there for a moment.

I got the shovels out of the truck, and Jerry got up, wiped the back of his hand across his bloody mouth, and we unloaded the body. Together, we carried the body until we find a brushy area. We cleared the brush and started digging. We dug and dug until we had a hole deep enough we had to leave an incline at one end to get up out of it. We crawled out and threw the body in and covered it. We put the brush back and used limbs to sweep our tracks back to the truck. We threw the limbs in the brush and the shovels in the back and get in.

Jerry sat at the wheel for a moment, and finally he said, "I am sorry."

I said, "Me too Jerry, me too." We drove back to the plantation house, and as I got out of the truck, I turned to Jerry and I told him, "We are square. We go on as if nothing happened. I tell my wife you came and got me because we had a tractor break down, and Gary got called back to the ship unexpectedly, and he will be back to get his stuff later. You go home and talk to Esther and tell her if she tells anyone, we will pin the murder on her. This never happened."

Nine months later, Joseph was born. Gary was still at sea, everyone thought, and no one was in jail.

I was speechless. I gathered myself, and as I prepared to speak, I heard Grandpa take a gasping breath and then he died. I got up and approached the bed. Grandpa was laying there with his eyes open, and his hands were clasped together.

I slid my hand over his face and closed his eyes. I took his hands in mine, and I said, "Goodbye, gramps."

When I went out to the living room, Thomas was sitting on the sofa, and he said, "He was waiting on you to get here so he could die."

I told Thomas I would call the funeral home and that he could go home now. "I will talk to you tomorrow, and we will settle up."

Thomas asked, "How did it go?" and I answered, "I came a day too early," and walked out the door.

CHAPTER 24

Reckoning

Cass has not said a word the whole time I was talking, and I had not really looked at her but rather toward her as I told the story. She comes into focus, and I see in her eyes that she can tell that I finally see her again. She asks, "Are you okay, John?"

I answer, "Yes, I am, actually I have never been better."

She says, "That is quite a story, not the kind of thing that anyone ever expects to hear. Do you think that he was looking for forgiveness?"

I say, "No, he just wanted me to know. It explained some things from my youth that he knew I sensed." I say, "The thing is, Joseph knew Jerry was not his father. That is where his anger came from."

Joseph heard his mom and Jerry arguing one night when he was eight years old. He had come in the back door through the kitchen, and they were in the living room going at it and did not hear him come in. Jerry broke Joseph's heart that day when Joseph heard him say, "That brat of yours doesn't even look like me. He looks like his father. Too bad he will never meet him."

Joseph went back out the back door and down to the pond where he cried until he could cry no more. He made a promise to himself that day that he would never cry again—a promise that he kept until the day he told me this story. It was the day we buried his mother.

Jerry had been gone for a few years before Esther passed away. From the time that Jerry died, Joseph took care of his mom. I was the sheriff in Raleigh, and Joseph worked at a furniture-making factory a few miles from the plantation and lived with his mother.

At the graveside as we laid his mom to rest, Joseph said to me, "Jerry was not my father." He said it very matter-of-factly, but there were tears in his eyes.

Of course, I already knew this, but I said, "What do you mean Jerry was not your father?" I knew they had never gotten along, and I was thinking that it was a statement of how he felt about Jerry. I looked at him and waited for an answer.

He stared right through me as he said, "My mom slept with some other guy, and he is my father."

I said, "How do you know this?" He relayed the story of over-hearing Jerry and his mom to me, and I said, "I am sorry, Joseph."

Joseph said, "I did not tell you so you would feel sorry for me. They never told me, but I told you because I think I know who it was." I waited for him to tell me, and when he did, I was astounded at what he said.

Joseph glared at me and said, "I think it was your dad."

I clenched my fist and stepped back far enough to get a good shot on him, and my brother Ron stepped in and asked, "What's going on here, you two?"

I told him to step aside, but he held his ground and said, "I don't care what it is. This is not the place for it. You two have been fighting your whole lives. Take a break."

I turned my back on Joseph and started to walk away. I stopped and turned back to him and said, "You are wrong." I didn't give him a chance to speak, and I left him and my brother standing by his mom's casket. I got in my truck and headed back to Raleigh.

From that point on, my brother dealt with Joseph as far as the affairs of care taking the old plantation until we were ready to sell it. My brother never asked me what I meant, and I never spoke to Joseph again until I called him to tell him where to leave the key and when I was coming to close the affairs of the property.

My brother Ron lives in Arizona, and we seldom talk or see each other. We get along fine, we just live in different worlds.

Cass looks at me incredulously and says, "This should be an interesting day then. Are you sure you want to see Joseph today, John?"

I say, "Yes, I am. He is a suspect, and I am a cop today. Let's saddle up and visit Joseph."

She looks at me and says, "Are you gonna punch him?"

I laugh and say, "Probably."

Cass says, "Remember you are a cop today."

I laugh and say, "Party pooper."

Cass says, "Let's get to the cruiser and get on out to Joseph's place." Dixie is waiting on us.

The tapestry maker is fast at work.

CHAPTER 25

The House Next Door

The drive out to Joseph's house is filled with light conversation about sports and hobbies as we get to know each other better.

Dixie lays patiently in the backseat until we pull onto the road that goes back to Joseph's house. The closer we get to the house, the more agitated she is getting. I look back and reach out to pet her, but she is pressed up against the back of the seat. I say, "What's wrong, girl?" and she gives me a whimper.

Cass says, "That is odd."

I say, "Obviously she has been here, and the memory is not good."

Cass pulls up by the garage and shuts the cruiser off. We sit there for a moment and survey the property. No one is out, and the place seems very quiet. There are no vehicles outside, but there could be in the garage. We step out of the vehicle, and I see Cass unsnap her gun but leave it in the holster.

I open the back door and wait on Dixie to hop out, but she does not move. I say, "Come on. girl." But she does not move. I coax her a bit, and she inches over to the open door and peaks out. Sensing no threat, she jumps down but stays right by my side.

All three of us walk up to the front door with me taking the lead. Now I unsnap my gun, and I knock on the door sharply. We wait. No one answers, so Cass steps up and raps again and yells "Sheriff's department, open up!" Still no answer.

Cass checks the door, and it is locked. She says, "Let's split up. You and Dixie check the garage, and I will go around the house."

I say, "Okay, but Dixie can go with you. She has a great nose and is a built-in alarm system."

Cass says, "Okay," and Dixie moves out in front of her.

I watch them ease their way around the house, and then I head for the garage. I check the side door, and it is locked so I go out front and pull up on the entrance doors. Both are locked. I go back to the side door, look around, and take my lock-pick set out of my pocket. I make quick work of picking the lock, and the door opens for me.

I check for a light switch. I find it, and to my surprise, the lights come on. I put my hand on my gun and look around the garage. It looks like any good old boy's garage. There are yard tools hanging on hooks and brackets, an old lawn mower is sitting in the corner, and I can see the pull cord is laying on top it. I inch my way into the garage, avoiding all the junk accumulated and filling the building.

It is obvious that no car has been stored in here for a long time. There is dust and cobwebs everywhere, and it looks as though no one has been in here for quite a while. Even though it is a two-car garage, I can see the whole room, and there is really no place to hide so I do a quick walkthrough, find nothing of interest and decide to go out and find the girls.

I turn the lights off and exit the garage and head over to the house to look for the girls. I remember I did not lock the door, and as I turn back to lock it, I hear Cass yell, "Hey, John, you done fooling around in the garage yet?"

I holler back, "Yes, nothing of interest in there anyway." I lock the door and make my way around the house.

Cass and Dixie make quite the pair as I watch them working together. Dixie is moving back and forth in front of Cass sniffing, ears erect as she seems to be taking her work seriously. Cass sees me and says, "I checked the back door and all the windows. Everything is locked up as far as I can tell."

I ask her, "Do you see any reason we should go in to check on anyone's safety?"

She says, "John, I know what you are thinking, but I think we need to stay out of the house. I don't want to ruin a potential case with an illegal entry." She also says, "I saw how you got in the garage, John."

I blush a bit and say, "I thought I saw movement in there."

She laughs and says, "Everwhat, don't do it again."

I say, "Yes, sheriff."

She says, "Let's go out and check that out building over there and the trail coming out of the woods behind it."

We work our way across the yard and up to the building. Dixie starts to get a little agitated again as she sniffs around the building. Cass and I walk up to the door. Cass checks it and finds it locked. She looks at me, and I raise my palms as if to say, "What you want me to do?"

We walk slowly around the building and Cass tries to look into the dirty windows but is unable to see anything through them. Dixie is really agitated now and has her tail tucked, and her ears are down. I walk over to her and pet her. She seems unable to calm down but follows me to the corner of the building, and as I turn to go behind it, she lays straight down and whines.

I turn the corner, and I see a ramshackle dog house with a rotten roof and a log chain anchored to a metal stake set in the ground. At the end of the chain is a dog collar that has been broken. I walk back around the edge of the building and kneel down by Dixie and say, "This was home, wasn't it?"

Dixie whimpers and I lift her head up and push the fur around her neck back and forth and I see the scars for the first time where the collar had been pulled against for who knows how long. I tell her, "No one will hurt you again, girl."

Cass has been watching, and she looks at me with knowing eyes as I pet Dixie. She gives me a moment and says, "Come over here and take a look at these tracks, John."

I stand up and so does Dixie, and we head over to where Cass is by the trail. I see the tracks right away, and I say, "They could be the same as the ATV tracks behind the pond, but I cannot be positive."

Cass says, "Time to try out those boots, sheriff. Let's take a hike."

I say, "Come on, Dixie, lead the way." Dixie takes the lead, nose to the ground, and Cass and I follow.

As we walk Cass says, "Tell me about your brother, John."

I say, "His name is Ron, he lives in Arizona, and he is a CNC programmer."

Cass says, "Wow, that is a lot of information to process all at once." She stops and says, "Tell me about your brother."

I say, "He is still alive, and I have never punched him."

Cass laughs and says, "That is a good start. Now one more time, tell me about your brother."

CHAPTER 26

Barns, Fish, and Family

I ask Cass, "Why are you so interested in my brother?"

She answers me, "Because your mother died in childbirth having you. You did say he was younger, didn't you?"

I smile and say, "Yes, I did."

Cass says, "Okay, one more time, tell me about your brother."

I say, "Yes, sheriff, let me tell you a tale of two brothers."

Ron was the son of a fishing family that lived just up the coast from the plantation. Hs parents both were lost at sea in a storm, presumed drowned. Ron was staying with an aunt who was in a quilting club with my grandma. His aunt's health was not good, but there was no one else to take care of him, and she was sharing that with Grandma.

That night, when she got back to the house from quilting club, she told my father about Ron and his situation. Dad told Grandma he wanted to pray and think about it. He said goodnight to Grandma but did not go to bed; he walked out by the pond, and I followed him.

He sat down on the bench that he had made for my mom, closed his eyes, bowed his head, and folded his hands. I stayed back in the bushes and watched him. He did not move for a long time. With his eyes still closed, he started talking, and I wondered who he was talking to, so I moved closer.

I heard him say, "We always talked about two kids, and there is this little fellow who needs a family down the road from the plantation, honey, and I am not sure what I should do. I wish you were here to talk to me and so we could make this decision together."

It was then that I realized he was talking to Mom. I started to cry, and Dad turned toward where I was hiding and said, "Come here, John."

I came to him, and he sat me on his lap and said, "I come out here and talk to your mom whenever I need to make a decision, John."

I didn't say anything, but the crying had stopped. He wiped my eyes and said, "How do you feel about having a little brother, John?"

I said, "It sounds cool, Dad."

He laughed and said, "I just said to your mom that I did not know how you would feel about it. I guess I was worried about nothing."

I said, "I can order him around and make him do stuff for me."

Dad smiled and said, "How about just loving him like he was your own blood and teaching him all the cool stuff you do around here?"

I said what I always said to dad when he asked me to do something—I said, "Yes sir."

Dad petitioned the court, and we adopted Ron within a few weeks. The process was a lot easier back then, and the judge was Grandpa's friend. Ron moved in, and I called him my brother from that day on.

Cass looks at me and says, "Was that so hard?"

I laugh and say, "No, it wasn't. I love my brother, but we have not spent a lot of time together for a long time."

Cass says, "So it is guilt that keeps you from talking about him."

I answer, "Yes."

Cass takes my face in her hands and says, "Look at me, John." I look in her eyes, and she says, "It is clear to me that you are home for a lot of reasons, John. Is this one of them?"

I think for a moment, and in my mind's eye, I see Ron and I up in the haymow crawling through one of our hay tunnels, and I say, "Yes."

CHAPTER 27

Not Happy Trails

Cass turns from me, and we continue following the tracks of the ATV. As we move along, I realize we are moving steadily toward the plantation.

Dixie has her nose to the ground. She is moving back and forth in front of us when she stops and issues a quick bark. Cass and I move up to where she is waiting, and we find a cigarette butt on the ground. Cass picks it up, and I walk up, look at it, and see it is a Camel, unfiltered, just like the one by the barn. I think we can safely assume that the same person dropped both of them.

We continue following the trail, but the only clue that we find is the cigarette butt. The trail does, however, lead right to the back side of the pond. At this point, it looks as though the ATV has been set here for a while. We can see where someone got off of the ATV and walked away from it, so we follow those tracks—boot tracks just like the ones I saw when I regained consciousness by my truck. We can also see that there are tracks going both directions, so someone came and went from the ATV.

All three of us are in quiet tracking mode now. Dixie is sweeping back and forth in front of us, and I have taken the lead on the tracking. Cass is quite a way off to my side opposite the pond and slightly behind me. We are moving cautiously but only because we are looking for clues. This is a cold trail.

As we work our way along the trail, I see that we are headed for the plantation house. It is a fairly short distance to the house, and we get sight of it quickly, so I stop and look back to where we picked up the trail and realize that I cannot see the place we started from.

Interesting. I wonder if you can see the house from that vantage point and not be seen yourself.

I start moving again, and we are soon up by my truck. At this point, I realize two things: one, we never got my key made; and two, the tracks go right to where I was wacked on the head.

I tell Cass to stop, and I say, "Slowly I turn, step by step, inch by inch."

Cass says, "Are you Abbot or Costello?"

I grin and say, "More like Barney Fife."

She says, "This is where you got hit from behind, isn't it?"

I say, "Yes, my head feels fine, but my pride is still sore."

Cass says, "While you were following the boot tracks, I was following the tracks from where the ATV left the spot it was stopped at. It ran parallel to the boot tracks and then takes off toward that wooded area over there."

I look to where she is pointing, and it is the area where Dixie and I found the blood trail and where I think someone was picked up by the ATV. The plot thickens. It would appear there are at least a couple of players in the game besides me.

Why would one of them attack me and then, it appears, one of them attack the other? When you take in to account the body on the beach, it also appears one of them was killed by the other.

The three of us follow the boot prints to the wooded area, and they do stop where the ATV stopped. And they end there also. I review my trek to the ocean with Cass, and we decide to head back to Joseph's house and her vehicle.

Cass spots a big tree stump and says, "Let's sit a moment and get a little water in us." She pulls two water bottles out of her pack, and we take a seat beside each other and open our bottles of water.

I ask Dixie, "Are you thirsty, girl?" and she runs over to me. Cass pours water in my cupped hands, and Dixie slurps some up. We sit quietly for a bit as Dixie continues to sniff the area.

As we sip our water and rest, I notice a glint off of something laying in the grass a little ways away from the spot where the ATV stopped. I stand up, and Cass must have seen it too because she gets up at the same time, and we walk over to it together.

Cass says, "Let me get an evidence bag and a glove on, John." She bends over and picks it up. It is a shell casing. Cass looks it over and says, "9mm."

I agree with her, and we decide to get moving. Cass bags the shell casing, and we set out for Joseph's house. We make great time as we move along quickly and with little talking. When we come into sight of the house, we slow our approach down as we look to see if anyone has arrived since we left. It appears that all is as we left it.

We get to her vehicle, Cass unlocks it. Dixie relieves herself and jumps in the open back door and takes her place, then I do the same in the front passenger seat as Cass gets in on her side. We buckle up and Cass says, "What the heck have you walked into here John?"

I laugh and say, "Retirement is overrated, anyway. Can I drive?"

Cass gives me her best stern look and says, "No."

I say, "You are no fun," and she says, "I am the most fun person I know."

I grin and say, "How many people do you know?"

She says, "Not many."

I say, "And I rest my case."

She laughs and says, "You still can't drive." She suggests that we stop at the Ford Dealer and get my key made. I agree, and off we go. She turns onto the highway and heads for town.

I say, "You drive like a girl."

Cass grins and says, "And I cry at Hallmark movies, but I will still shoot you in the leg if you don't be quiet and let me drive."

I say, "Yes ma'am. I don't want to be shot today." We settle into our place of mutual respect and find our way back to town.

Cass pulls up in front of the Ford dealer, and I see the name is Braun Ford. I ask her, "Is this place owned by Sylvester Braun the Fourth?"

She laughs and says, "Yes. We call him B4."

I laugh and say, "I like it."

She asks "Do you know him?"

I say, "Oh yeah. My family and his are connected over the last hundred years."

Cass says, "I can't wait to hear this story." Then she stops and says, "I have to ask you…" and I interrupt and say, "No, I have never punched him."

We both laugh and get out of the cruiser and walk into the dealership. As soon as we enter the building, I see B4 coming toward us. He has that big ole car salesman smile on his face as he takes my hand and shakes it furiously and says, "John, John, John, it is so good to see you."

I have to grin as I say, "Sly, it is good to see you too."

Cass looks at me quizzically and Sylvester says, "No one calls me that anymore, John."

I grin and say, "Yeah, they do."

He ignores me and moves on to Cass. This is going to be fun. Before he can walk away, I ask him, "Hey, do you ever see Joseph anymore?"

He gets a funny look on his face and mutters, "Hardly ever."

I say, "Okay, we are looking for hm."

Sly does not respond to that but asks for the VIN code. I look at Cass and get the shoulder shrug response from her, but I think to myself, *Sly is holding back on us.*

CHAPTER 28

Brains or Braun

I give Sly the VIN code off of my truck, and he asks if we want to wait while they make me a key. I say yes and thank you. Sly starts to walk away but stops and looks back at me and says, "I don't like being called Sly."

I smile and say, "I would not like it either."

He starts to say something but thinks better of it and walks away. He hollers back over his shoulder, "Key will be ready in about a half hour!"

I walk back outside looking for Cass and find her talking to a deputy. Cass turns to me and says, "They identified the body on the beach. The name is Andy Jackman, and his last known address is up in Orangeburg area. His jacket says he is a bad man—was a bad man—and the slug they pulled from him was a 9mm. His rap sheet is long and nasty."

I say, "His nasty days are over, and I would think we can conclude he was shot on the plantation and transported from the scene."

I tell her we have a half hour until the key is ready, and Cass says, "Tell me about the Brauns."

I see a café across the street and suggest we go over for a cup of coffee, and Cass agrees. We let Dixie out of the SUV for a moment to do her business, put her back in, and walk over to the café. We choose an outside table, and a waitress takes our order for two black coffees promptly as we are seated. We settle in, and Cass says, "Okay, cowboy, let's hear it."

I tell her that the Brauns came to America in the early 1800s. They were a shipping company family, and they transported slaves to America and cotton and indigo back to England.

At that time, South Carolina had about 10 percent of the slaves in America—around four hundred thousand of them. On the plantations that produced indigo, the life expectancy of the slaves who worked the indigo was about seven years. Indigo and cotton were in great demand in England at that time so with the need for new slaves and the demand for cotton and indigo, the Brauns made big profits off of the American plantation owners.

Before the war of 1812, Thomas Jefferson imposed a shipping embargo that crippled the economy of the coastal states. The Brauns were able to maintain and increase their profits by becoming smugglers. The family has always been willing to ship or move things for anyone willing to pay for their services. They were known for transporting Irish immigrants to America. The ships used to bring the Irish here during the potato blight that ravaged Ireland and caused the starvation of over a million Irish were called "coffin ships," as many died on them or had to be quarantined when they got to New York because of disease and malnutrition.

In doing this, they shipped the Irish gangs to America that would run New York City. They did not care about wars or sides, only who would pay the most. They would ship anything if you were willing to pay for it.

In 1865, when Union troops arrived in South Carolina and informed the slaves they were free, everything changed again. The cotton industry lost its free labor and was being affected by imports from other countries, and the wooden ships were becoming obsolete as the iron hull steam freighters were taking over international shipping. They could handle far more weight and were faster and consistent.

The Brauns were being pushed out of shipping, so they tried their hand at a legal endeavor. They invested in a cotton industry at exactly the wrong time. People were leaving South Carolina in huge numbers, especially what they thought would be the cheap labor—the blacks. There was no one to work in the factory they invested in in Charleston, and to top it off, in 1886, an earthquake registering 7.3 destroyed the factory and most of Charleston.

The Brauns went back to what they did best—anything illegal. The head of the family, Sylvester Braun, went to New York and established an alliance with one of the Irish gangs there, The Dead Rabbits. Even though the Iron Clads had taken over the shipping lanes, the wooden boats still served a purpose. They would ship anything—especially if the name Braun was attached.

The harbors were controlled by the gangs, and the Brauns came and went with protection of the Gangs. At the advent of WWI, the Brauns smuggled items designated for the war in this country as their ships were now obsolete.

By this time, Sylvester Braun the Second was a young man and following in his father's footsteps. When the 18th amendment was passed, and the prohibition was announced, it opened a whole new area of smuggling—liquor. That is where my grandpa and the Brauns crossed paths. They were bringing liquor down the coast and needed a place to bring it into South Carolina.

"The cove I told you about was perfect. My grandfather formed a partnership with Sylvester Braun the Second and saved the plantation which had long ago stopped making any money. He paid off the local law and made huge amounts of money for the thirteen years that the prohibition lasted. When it ended, Grandpa broke ties with the Braun family, but they stayed in South Carolina. I did not find this out until later in my life. It answered many questions I had as a youth but also raised many more.

"I did, however, find out where Jerry came from. The Irish sent him here with the Brauns because he had killed another gang leader in New York. He owed Grandpa, so he was loyal to him, but Grandma never trusted Jerry. There is much more that I could tell you, but I think that is enough for you to get the idea."

I stop and take a deep breath and realize I had never told anyone that stuff before. Cass sees the look in my eyes and says, "Wow."

I smile and say, "My dad and B4's dad were about the same age, so I grew up with B4, but we called him Sly."

Cass says, "I am at a loss for words, John."

I say, "Me too." We finish our coffee in silence. The waitress comes over and I pay for the coffee and to my surprise, Cass lets me.

As we get up to go, Cass puts her hand on mine, sending a shock though my body, looks in my eyes, and says, "You really should write a book about your life."

I look deep into her eyes and say, "I am still waiting for the happy ending."

Cass smiles and says something that would change me: "Perhaps you should be looking for a happy beginning instead, John."

CHAPTER 29

Don't Change the Station

I follow Cass back across the street to Braun's Ford. I think about how stagnant my life had become since my retirement and the success of the book. Suddenly, I was living again.

I have a tattoo on my right shoulder of the Greek word *kairos*. In the Greek, there are two words for time. One is *chronos* meaning chronological or sequential time. The other is *kairos* which means real, critical or opportune moment. I was living in a kairos moment. I had been living a chronos lifestyle for too long. Another interpretation of kairos is new beginning or a time for action.

I stop, look up, and I say out loud, "Thank you."

Cass turns and says, "Who are you talking to?"

I answer, "Dad."

She says, "Which one?" and I answer, "Both of them."

She grins and says, "You never cease to surprise me, John Young."

I grin back at her and say, "I might say the same thing about you, Cass."

We both laugh and head into the dealership. I hold the door for Cass, and she says, "Quite the gentleman."

I do my fake hat tip, and we walk up to the parts counter together. The parts man's name tag reads Al, so I ask, "How is the key coming, Al?"

Al says, "It is ready, sir."

I say, "Please call me John."

Al says, "As you wish, sir."

I laugh, but Al does not flinch. I look at Cass, and she just shrugs her shoulders. I ask Al how much I owe, and he says, "Mr. Braun said to tell you no charge."

I say, "Oh no, I insist on paying."

He says, "Mr. Braun said not to accept your money, sir."

I laugh again and say, tongue in cheek, "Okay, sir."

Big Al hands me the key and says, "Thank you and have good rest of the day, sir."

I start to respond in kind but say, "Tell Sly thank you."

Again, Al does not flinch, and I turn to walk away. Before I can get a step in, I hear Al say, "My uncle does not like being called that."

I turn back smile and say, "I know."

As Cass and I walk out she says, "That was interesting."

I grin and say, "This whole trip has been nothing but interesting."

Cass says, "Never a dull moment with you around, John Young." When we get back in the cruiser, Cass says, "We need to go to the station and check in."

I say, "Great, I want to see where you work."

Cass and I talk a little more about the Brauns as we make our way the few blocks back to the station. When we arrive at the station, I say, "Why don't I get Dixie out for a quick stretch and a bathroom break while you check in, and I will be in in a little bit?"

Cass says, "Sounds good," and she heads up the steps into the station.

I open the door to let Dixie out and realize I don't have a leash. I open the door and say, "Okay girl, don't run off."

She tilts her head and looks at me like she thinks it is more likely that I will do something stupid before she does. She hops out and we find a nice piece of grass and she starts sniffing. As I am standing there, I hear a female voice from behind me say, "John Young, is that you?"

I turn, and there stands my high school sweetheart, Patty Metcalf. She says, "Are you just going to stand there, or are you going to say hello, John?"

I say, "I am sorry, Patty, you caught me off guard."

I just get "hello" out, and she says, "Give me a hug." But before I can respond, she has me in a way too personal hug. As I try to disengage myself from her grasp, I look over her shoulder to see Cass standing on the steps of the station, watching us. I separate from Patty and holler for Cass to come over.

Cass walks up and asks, "Who is your friend, John?"

I say, "This is Patty Metcalf, a friend from high school."

She says, "John, you are being too modest." As she extends her hand to Cass, she says, "John and I were an item in high school, and the last name is now Braun."

I look at Cass, and it is all we can do to not laugh out loud. I say, "We were just at the dealership," and Patty says, "I know, I just came from there myself. Sylvester told me you were there. I think he is a little jealous of you, John."

"I don't know why he would be jealous of me," I say. "He is wealthy, handsome, and has a beautiful wife, and I am just a retired cop who lives all alone."

"That may be," Patty says, "but he has been talking about you for the last two days, John."

I look at Cass, and I see the knowing look in her eyes. She and I know that no one knew I was here until last night when I checked in to the motel. I don't mention that to Patty, but I do ask her if she knows Joseph, and she answers, "Yes, he was just at our place a couple days ago."

I say, "Joseph, the son of Jerry from the plantation," and she says, "Of course, John. I have known him my whole life. He helps Sylvester with things."

I ask, "What kind of things?"

She says, "Whatever needs doing."

I say, "That is kind of vague, Patty."

She says, "If you need to know more, ask Sylvester. I don't pay much attention to his business."

I say, "Yes, we will be doing that. In the meantime, please tell Sly about our conversation. I would not want him to get the wrong idea."

She says, "Yes I will, and John, he hates being called that."

I smile and say, "Yeah, I have heard that before."

*****

As we walk back to put Dixie in the cruiser, Cass says, "Now let me check my facts here. You said the only person who knew you were coming was Joseph and he was not expecting you for at least three more days and I just heard Sly tell you that he seldom saw Joseph, but his wife says that Joseph works for him, and it would appear that Sly knew you were here already."

"That is correct," I say.

Cass says, "I see why you call him Sly."

I grin and say, "Now you know why we called him Sly and not Slick." Cass laughs when I tell her, "When he was young, he thought it was a compliment."

We get to the top of the steps, and Cass opens the door as we walk into the station. I step in and it seems like everyone has stopped what they were doing and are just looking at us. Cass says, "Does anyone here have any work to do or what?" Everyone quickly gets back on task, and Cass says, "Let's go to my office."

On the way, she goes by a deputy's desk and tell him to be in her office in five minutes. We step into the office, and Cass says, "Have a seat, cowboy."

I say, "Thank you, ma'am, don't mind if I do." I take a seat in a chair that is already in front of her desk and settle in.

Cass goes around and takes her place of authority on the other side of the desk, and I feel like a kid in the principal's office. We are both laughing as the deputy opens the door and walks in.

Cass looks up as he enters and sternly says, "Jim, what does it mean when the door to my office is closed?"

"It means knock, sheriff," he says.

She says, "Did you?"

He says, "No, sheriff, my apologies."

Cass says, "Jim, this is Sheriff John Young. He is assisting me on this case."

I stand up and shake hands with Jim, and he says, "I know who you are, sir. I read the book."

Cass says, "Okay, Jim, if you are done sucking up, what have you got for us on the body?"

I take my seat, and Jim opens the folder he is carrying and goes over the coroner's report with us. The estimated time of death falls right in line with the events at the plantation and the rest of the information we already knew.

Cass thanks Jim, and he shakes my hand again and says, "It is a pleasure to meet you, sir."

I tell him, "Thank you and nice to meet you, deputy."

As he leaves the office, Cass gets a phone call. I wait and listen, but I can't tell much from the part of the call I am listening to. She hangs up and says, "That was one of my deputies, John. I called him when we first got here and told him to take a plain car over and watch the dealership and see if Mr. Braun left. He just left, and my guy is tailing him."

I look at her and say, "Perhaps I should be calling you Slick."

She smiles and says, "Never underestimate me, John."

I say, "You have no worries there. I can already see you are a force to be reckoned with, and I am glad we are on the same side." I ask her, "What do we do next sheriff?"

She answers, "We don't change the station."

I say, "Okay, but what the heck does that mean?"

She grins and says, "We keep doing what we are doing, and we turn the volume up a little."

I laugh and say, "I love this song. How about a duet?"

She says, "Sonny and Cher, The Captain and Tennille, Peaches and Herb."

I say, "They were all good, but I was thinking my favorite new duo—us."

Cass says, "They must be new."

I grin and say, "Yes, but they have a fresh new sound, and they have a unique chemistry."

Cass says, "I can't wait to see if they are a success."

"Me too," I say.

Cass says, "Let's go turn up the volume."

CHAPTER 30

Lightning and Thunder

Cass turns the shell casing in as evidence and tells the deputy that she gives it to, "We need to check for prints and run them right away if you get any."

The deputy takes the evidence bag and says, "Yes ma'am."

Cass says, "Call me as soon as you have any info." Once again, she gets a "yes ma'am" from the deputy. She turns to me and says, "Let's take another drive."

Tongue in cheek, I say, "Yes ma'am."

I get a sideways glance but no response as she heads for the door. I follow her out to the SUV, and we get in our opposite sides. Cass says, "There is a biker club on the edge of town that I think we need to go visit."

I say, "Sounds like fun."

Cass says, "They call themselves The Skulls."

We pull up in front of the club in the county vehicle and find a couple of tough-looking fellas sitting on a bench underneath of the front awning. They both get up slowly from their seats and take a menacing walk toward our vehicle. Cass and I step out of the SUV and move toward them.

They get too close to Cass, and she says, "You guys don't smell good enough to stand that close to me."

The blond-haired biker says, "Listen here sweetie, you don't talk to a man like that."

Cass says, "If you see a man around here anywhere, let me know, and I will respect him."

The other biker laughs and says to his buddy, "She has some spunk."

He looks over at me and says, "What about the cowboy there? Does he qualify?"

Cass says, "Ask him yourself."

The one turns to me and the other one stays facing Cass. The one that turns to me moves over closer to me and says, "You don't look so bad."

I say, "Thanks I just got a haircut."

The biker says, "That's not the kind of bad I meant."

I say, "Oh, I'm sorry, I thought you were complimenting me."

He moves a little closer and says, "Don't talk to me like I am stupid."

I say, "Okay, I will talk to you like you are smart. Could you explain the problem-solving principal of Occam's razor to me?"

He moves toward me, fists up, and Cass says, "I hate to interrupt this good-natured exchange of intellect, but we are looking for someone."

The blond says, "We don't know them."

Cass says, "I did not say a name yet."

The second guy says, "It don't matter." We don't talk to cops, and we ain't snitches."

Cass says, "We are looking for Joseph McDougal."

I see the look in both of their eyes, and it is obvious they know something. Cass says to them, "We need to take a look inside."

The blond one says, "This is private property."

Cass says, "So invite us in then."

The second one says, "You two are welcome to go in if you can get by us."

I look over at Cass, and she says, "They are pretty big, John."

I say, "Yep. they are, but what the heck, I am kind of bored."

The second guy lunges at me, and I sidestep him and drop him with a hard right cross on the left temple.

The blond turns, looks at Cass, and says, "My turn," just as Cass tases him.

I laugh and say, "Is it thunder before lightning or is it lightning before thunder?" I walk lean over number two thug and say, "You probably know."

He squints up at me and says, "He ain't here, man."

I ask, "Where did he go?"

They both say, "We don't know."

Cass looks at me and says, "Do you believe them?"

"Only the part that he is not here, but I imagine that is the only truth we are going to get out of them."

She agrees, and we get back in the SUV. Cass says, "You been waiting to hit someone all day so patiently."

I say, "It was just a matter of time."

Cass laughs and says, "I love this channel. The hits just keep coming." We look at each other and laugh hard.

The two goons outside the SUV give us the finger, we wave goodbye, and off we go.

"Next stop?" I ask Cass.

She says, "It's a surprise."

I say, "I hate surprises."

Cass says, "Yeah, I know."

CHAPTER 31

No Take Out Today

Cass is unusually quiet as we drive toward the coast. I try to engage her a couple of times, but she just gives me superficial answers as we cruise along. We are about eight miles out of town, and you can smell the ocean now. Cass says, "Right over this crest is where she lives."

I don't say anything and choose to let her lead this venture. She turns off the two-lane on to a stone drive, and I can see a nice little bungalow on a hill overlooking the ocean. She pulls up to the house and shuts off the SUV.

Dixie and I are both waiting for her to say something, but she just gets out of the vehicle and says, "What are you two waiting on?"

I hop out and open the back door of the SUV, and Dixie hops out. Dixie lets me rub her head, and she runs toward the bungalow.

I look up and see a pretty older woman who looks a lot like Cass. Dixie runs straight to her and sits right at her feet. The woman bends over and grabs her face and says, "You are a fine-looking specimen of the Carolina dog family."

Dixie gives her a woof but continues to sit at her feet. The woman says to Dixie, "Go bring your man here." Dixie gives another "woof" and runs up to me and dances around me a moment then gives a tug on my pant leg. I say, "Okay, girl, I heard her."

With Dixie out in front, I make my way up the porch where Cass and the lady are embracing. They release each other, laughing, and Cass says, "Sheriff John Young, this is my mother Joann Quince."

I take off my hat and extend my hand, which she firmly shakes, and I say, "It is a pleasure, ma'am."

She smiles a smile that would light a small planet and says, "I am so pleased to make your acquaintance, John." She looks me up and down and says, "You are right, Cass, he is good-looking in a rugged way, but your father was the best-looking man I ever met."

I watch them as they smile at each other as the memories race through their minds, and I realize that they are both looking at me. Cass says, "Hey there, cowboy, what are you thinking?"

I say, "Cass, I thought you might be the most stunning woman I have ever met until right now."

Cass and her mom both laugh at me as her mom asks, "Is he always such a sweet talker?"

Cass says, "By sweet talker, do you mean is he always full of crap? Yeah, he is."

I grin and say, "I know when I have been insulted."

Cass laughs and says, "There's a first time for everything."

I say, "Little Texas, 1992."

Her mom says, "From the album, *First Time for Everything*."

Cass says, "This is exactly what I expected of you two."

Her mom says, "So then we are right on track. Let's go in the house and eat lunch. You two go wash up, and I will get lunch ready for the four of us."

I ask, "Who else is coming?"

Joann says, "Dixie."

Cass leads me to a mud room off the porch, and Joann and Dixie head into the kitchen. As we are washing up, I ask her, "Why didn't you tell me your mom lived here?"

She says, "You didn't ask."

I have no good come back for that, so I don't say anything. We dry our hands, and I follow her into the kitchen where I see Dixie eating from a very nice bowl beside the kitchen table. Joann says, "Take a seat there by Dixie, John, and Cass, you sit across the table from John."

I say, "Yes ma'am, and thank you."

Cass says, "Why the seating designation, mother?"

Joann says, "Could you just do what I ask please?"

Cass does not respond but takes her place across from me. I am watching her mom as she surveys her domain. She is staging the room so that she can observe our interaction and our body language as we have lunch. Smart woman. I like her.

I say, "Joann, you have a lovely home and a great view here."

She says, "It is wonderful, isn't it?" I am looking out the huge bay window that looks out at the beach and ocean, and I am thinking to myself, *I wonder how she can afford this*, when she says with a lilt in her voice, "My late husband's family owned this home for years and left it to us when they passed. Does that answer your question?"

I grin and say, "I did not ask one."

She says, "Not with words." I am impressed, and she knows it. I even like that. I ask her what we will be having for lunch and she says, "Stimulating conversation and food."

Cass says, "If you two are done flirting, I would like to eat, Mom." Her mom's laugh was melodic and unrestrained, and I could see the smile that appeared on Cass's face as she listened to it. Cass says, "I asked Mom to make her Charleston-style shrimp and grits and sautéed greens."

Her mom says, "And that is what we will be having for our entrée after an arugula, peach, shaved red onion, and candied pecan salad with a Dejon Vinaigrette with champagne vinegar. But the first thing we will be having is a prayer to bless this meal and this time together." She looks at me and says, "John."

I look in those eyes and know that my only option is "Yes ma'am." I say, "Let's bow our heads and pray." I say, "God, thank you for this day, this food, and this time together, in Jesus name, Amen."

When I open my eyes, I see tears on Joann's cheeks. I ask her, "Did I say something wrong?"

She says, "No, John, your prayer was perfect. It reminded me of the simple way that Bill, my late husband, prayed. It has been a long time since a man prayed at this table. John Young, you are welcome in my home. Let's eat and talk of ships and sealing wax, of cabbages and kings."

I say, "I cannot help myself and so I must reply, the sea was wet as wet could be, the sands were dry as dry. You could not see a cloud because no cloud was in the sky."

Joann looks at Cass, not me, and says, "Oh my, this should prove to be an interesting lunch."

Cass says, "As long as he doesn't punch somebody."

I say, "They all had it coming."

Joann says, "Now, Cass, I am sure they did."

Cass says, "Don't encourage him, Mom!"

Joann laughs as she excuses herself from the table and says, "I will be right back with the salad, and you can start telling me all about yourself and how you two met."

Cass says, "This is not a date, Mom."

As she leaves the room Joann says, "Could have fooled me."

CHAPTER 32

No Leftovers

By the time the meal was over, we had shared in a way that I did not think was possible. The food was fantastic, but the women were amazing.

I have always been at ease meeting new people, but it was because I never shared anything personal. I made myself bullet-proof emotionally. I wore my emotional armor to keep from being assaulted by my feelings just like I wore body armor to protect from being assaulted by bullets. I find myself in new territory, as yet, unexplored. The final frontier, going where no John has gone before. You get the idea. This was uncomfortable but exhilarating.

As Cass and I say our goodbyes, her mom takes my hands and says, "Please come back again, John, you are always welcome in my home." I thank her, and to my surprise, I hug her.

As Cass and I walk to the SUV with Dixie close behind, she takes my hand in hers for just a moment and squeezes it then releases it. I have a feeling she is in new territory also, so I say not a word.

Cass's phone rings just as we are getting in the SUV, and as she answers, I put Dixie in the back, and I took my place in the passenger seat. Cass finishes talking and hangs up. She looks over at me and says, "Braun is at Joseph's house. Let's go."

Cass pulls out of her mom's driveway and heads back up the coast. She keeps her eyes on the road as she says, "You and Mom sure got on well."

I say, "She is a vital intelligent and intriguing woman."

Cass says, "I agree. After Dad was killed, Mom took over. She took the large life insurance policy payment and invested very wisely so she could stay home and raise me. We were by no means wealthy, but we could afford anything we needed. Mom taught me to live within my means and to work hard.

"When I reached high school age, Mom went to work because she wanted to. She had been taking classes on grief counselling and went to work for a small family-owned Christian counselling center. She worked three days a week until five years ago. Now she volunteers and does charity work all over the county."

I ask, "Did she ever remarry?"

"No, she did not," Cass replies. "Many men have pursued her, but she just was not interested. When I got older and our relationship matured, I was able to ask her why. She told me until she could just accept a man for who he was and not compare them to Dad. It was not fair to them. Evidently, she never got to that point or eventually no longer cared, I don't know. What I do know is she is very much at peace with her life. I never hear her complain, and I only see her smile. She appreciates each day and lives it to the fullest."

Just then her phone rings again, and when she was finished talking, she says, "There is another cop meeting us at Joseph's place."

I ask, "Who is it?"

Cass says, "The deputy did not say his name, just that he had a vested interest in this case."

I think on this for a moment but decide—who cares? I will know in a little while anyway. As we drive, I am going over the information we have up to this point and organizing the events in my mind, trying to think if I am leaving anything out of the sequence, when Cass says, "We are almost there."

I look up and see we are coming up on the property, and I see a Lincoln Navigator in the driveway. As we pull in, the front door opens and out walks B4.

Cass and I step out and I open the back door for Dixie to get out and she looks out the door but does not get out. I say, "Come on, girl, what's the matter?"

Dixie whines a little but hops out of the SUV. She stays close to me as we move toward the house. B4 stands by the door and waits on us. When we get up to him, he asks, "What are you two doing here?"

Cass asks, "We wonder the same thing about you, Mr. Braun."

He says to Cass, "Mr. Braun. So professional."

She says, "You changed our relationship when you lied to us, Mr. Braun."

He feigns having no idea what she means when he says, "And what did I lie about?"

Cass says, "Your relationship with Joseph."

Before he can answer, an old Chevy step-side truck pulls in the driveway. We all turn to look and see who it is. I can't see through the window tint, but the truck seems familiar to me. The door opens and out steps Buck Branson.

I look at Cass and say, "You knew."

She says, "Yes, I did."

I say, "I will deal with you later."

Cass tells B4 not to leave, and we walk over to Buck. Though he is a big man, he is a fit man. I see he still has that easy smile, and he moves like a man that is at ease in his skin and his place in life.

I extend my hand, and he takes it firmly in his, does not shake but holds me firmly in front of him and looks me over. I don't say anything but wait on him to speak.

When his appraisal is over, he shakes my hand and says, "You look good, John."

I say, "Thank you, sheriff, you look great for your age."

He laughs and says, "For my age, huh. I see you still don't know how to give a proper compliment."

I laugh and see he has turned his attention to Cass. She walks up to him, and they hug. I say, "How long has this been going on?"

Cass says, "Since the day he hired me." Cass says, "Who do you think I replaced, John?"

I think about it and realize I had never considered it. What a homecoming this has been so far.

Buck walks over to B4 and says, "Sly, how you are doing?"

I have seen that look in the eyes of my prey many times. Sly was in trouble, and he knew it. Most types of prey are most dangerous when cornered. To assume Sly was any different would be a mistake.

The three of us make a semi-circle around him, and Cass says, "Okay, Sly, time to answer some questions truthfully."

Sly surprises me when he grins and says, "Of course, how could I say no to such an esteemed team of officers? I didn't get to the top by being afraid."

Buck says, "The cream always rises to the top, but so does the crap. Which one are you Sly?"

Cass says, "Why don't we go in the house to talk, Sly?"

Sly says, "Why not?"

I tell Dixie to stay, and we enter the house. I look around me, and my heart skips a beat.

"What the heck is this?" Cass asks.

Buck looks around the room and says, "Scary."

Cass says, "Yeah, it is."

I can't speak. I look at Sly, and he is grinning ear to ear. He looks at me and says, "Welcome home, John."

CHAPTER 33

A Picture Tells a Thousand Stories

I am just standing there, stunned, when Buck says, "Sly, did you know about this?"

Sly says, "You mean the pictures? Yeah, kind of creepy, isn't it?" and laughs.

As I look around the room, I see most of my childhood and young adult life wallpapering the living room. There are pictures of me, my brother, Grandma, and Grandpa and Dad, all black and white and covering many years. They are tacked to the walls, and many of them are stained and have the bottoms rolled up from years of hanging there. Some of them have my face cut out of them, and some of them are slashed.

Cass asks, "Did he ever tell you why he has these, Sly?"

Sly grins and says, "Nope."

Cass asks, "Is this the first time you have ever been here?"

Sly says, "Nope."

Cass asks, "How many times have you been here?"

Sly says, "Not many."

Cass says, "That is not a number," and Sly says, "I know." Cass asks him, "Why are you here?" and Sly asks Cass, "Why are *you* here?"

Buck interrupts the give and take and says, "Enough, Sly. I know you are not going to tell us crap and anything you do tell us will be crap."

Sly grins but does not respond.

Cass says, "Let us tell you what we do know. We know that Joseph works for you, we know that you knew John was here before anyone else, even though no one knew he would be here when he got here early. John was assaulted on his property and that makes you a suspect. We know that you are worried about John being here for some reason."

Buck says to him, "And I know that you are a bottom feeder and the son of a bottom feeder but just smart enough to stay out of trouble."

I can see the anger in Sly's eyes as Buck is speaking, and he is clenching his fists but not speaking.

Buck says, "My whole life, I have watched your family hurt and use people, watched your family get wealthy off of other's misfortune and habits. It is about to get bad for you, Sly. You woke up the wrong sleeping dog.

"This man here, John Young, his bite is worse than his bark. As a matter of fact, he seldom barks before he bites. Now about this lady here. Make no mistake, Sheriff Quince here will light up your life in a heartbeat. Now as far for me. I am retired, I don't have a badge or any respect for you, so I basically have no rules to abide by. Do you get my drift, Sly?"

Sly is no longer grinning, and he is obviously mad. To my surprise, he pulls himself together and asks, "Am I under arrest?"

Cass says, "No, but don't leave town."

Sly says, "Then I am leaving."

Buck lets him get a few paces away and says, "Hey, Sly, we are coming for you."

Sly says, "Well, come on then, and I hate being called Sly."

Buck laughs and says, "I know!"

Sly gets in his truck and throws gravel as he leaves.

Buck watches him go and turns to Cass and me, grins from ear to ear, and says, "That was fun."

Cass laughs and says, "Great, now I have two retirees on the case. Next thing you know the AARP will send in an investigator. Looks like we should go back to the station and get vests and walkers."

I look at Buck and say, "I think she is insulting us."

Buck says, "Never mind her, she has a dry sense of humor."

I say, "Yeah, a lot of sheriffs are like that, I hear."

Buck says, "Yeah, I have heard that too."

Cass says, "Okay, are you two has been comedians done yapping?"

In unison, we both say, "Yes ma'am, we are."

Cass asks, "Buck, do you want to come back to the station and look at our evidence so far?"

Buck says, "Yes, if it is okay with you, sheriff?"

Cass says, "Yes sir, it would be great if you could give us some more background, and maybe you can keep John from punching everyone he meets."

Buck laughs and says, "He does have a nasty right hook."

Cass says, "I am going to take some pictures of this living room before I leave. John, you ride with Buck, and I will meet you two back at the station."

Once again, we say, "Yes ma'am." As we get in Buck's truck, Cass yells, "Could you two not get in trouble please?"

Buck says, "Us? Never."

I ask Buck, "Is this the truck you had when I graduated from college?"

He says, "Yep, she still runs great."

I ask, "Can't you afford a new one?"

Buck says, "Sure I can. That's not the reason I don't get one. I am faithful to people and things that are faithful and good to me. This truck has been a good one, and I have lots of memories in her. Plus, who do I have to impress anyway? When Penny passed, it was just me, this old truck, and my dog Buddy. Now Buddy is gone too. All I have left is this truck and memories."

I say, "My, that's a sad story. Are you done?"

Buck looks over at me and says, "No, let's go make some new memories."

I say, "What you got in mind?"

Buck says, "Let's stop at a little place on the coast that Joseph frequents."

I say, "We better tell Cass."

Buck says, "No, let's you and me have a little time together, John. Probably nothing there anyway."

Against my better judgement, I say, "Okay." Remember, I said against my better judgement.

CHAPTER 34

The Buck Stops Here

Buck pulls, does a U-turn. We pull out of the driveway and head south toward along the coast.

I say, "Buck, it is good to see you."

He says, "I have followed your career as much as could through news clips, your book, and the chatter among law enforcement people I know. You have not been home for a long time, John. What brings you back now, John?" I tell him I have decided to sell the plantation property. Buck says, "I am not surprised at all. It would seem that you have done everything you could to forget about the place."

I laugh and say, "Yep."

Buck says, "You always were a man of few words."

I say, "That was true."

Buck asks, "What do you mean?"

I hesitate for a moment, and Buck pulls the truck over to the side of the road puts it in park and says, "Let's hear about it."

I say, "It's a long story," and Buck says, "I got all kinds of time and so do you, John."

I laugh and say, "Just a couple of old retired guys talking."

Buck says, "Speak for yourself, I am not old."

I grin and say, "You do seem to have a lot of energy."

He says, "And don't you dare say for a man my age, John. Now quit stalling and tell me what's really going on with you."

I tell him that I have been alone for a long time, and I was quite comfortable in my solitude. I had no one to answer to, I go home when I want, and I go where I want and when I want. No one tells me what to do or eat, when to go to bed, or when to get up. I am not rich, but I have plenty of money. I can afford to travel when and where I want.

Buck stops me and says, "But you don't go anywhere, do you?"

I answer him, "No, I don't."

Buck says, "You still have not answered me."

"Well, I find myself thinking that I might not be as happy as I thought," I say.

Buck says, "My word, man, can't you just say what you are thinking?"

I take a breath and ask him, "Does Cass have a man in her life?"

Buck laughs hard and says, "Is that what this is all about? You are outside your comfort zone because you are finding out you actually do have feelings."

I would like to argue with him, but I know he is right. Buck smiles and pats me on the arm and says, "John, being alone is okay, and being with someone is okay. One is not better than the other. They are just different. Which one do you want to be?"

I say, "I think I want to try not being alone."

Buck says, "Then why are you telling me and not her?"

I say, "I will think about it, and thanks, Buck."

Buck pulls back on the road, and we travel in silence for about ten minutes. We turn down a gravel-and-sand driveway, and Buck pulls the truck over and stops. He says, "There is an old garage up around the bend there that Joseph and his buddies hang out at. I think we should walk up and not ruin the surprise."

I say, "I see you are still carrying, but can you still shoot?"

He laughs and says, "Let's hope you don't have to find out."

I say, "Let's hope he is here. I can't wait to say, 'The Buck stops here' to him." I try to maintain a serious look on my face, but Buck starts to laugh, and I can't help but join him.

When we settle down, Buck says, "Okay, John, let's move."

I say, "Just like the old days, sir." We start walking down the drive, and I can't help it. I say quietly "The Buck stops here."

Buck turns and says, "If you say that again, I will shoot you in the leg."

I say, "You would not shoot me, Buck." He does not respond, and I say, "You wouldn't, would you?"

He just keeps walking.

CHAPTER 35

Around the Bend

It seems awfully quiet as we make our way down the driveway. We turn the corner and see the garage at the bottom of the hill. There are a bunch of old cars and trucks sitting around, many with grass and weeds growing up around them. The property is unkempt, and well, let's just say it looks like it has been a long time since anyone cared about the upkeep. We see no sign of any activity, but there is a motorcycle parked in front of the garage.

Buck says, "Let's split up. You go around and come in from the north side, and I will come in from the south."

I agree with him, grab his arm, and say, "Be careful, Buck, I don't like the feel of this place."

Buck says, "Don't worry about me, John, I can take care of myself."

Just as he finishes his sentence, the report of a rifle barked, and a slug slammed into the tree beside his head, showering him with bark and splinters. I see his head is bleeding as the next slug whirs by us, and we duck for cover.

Behind the trees that we think separate us from the gunman, we gather our wits, and I tell Buck to let me look at his head. He says, "It's just a scratch."

I say, "Your scratch is bleeding pretty badly. Let me look at it."

I take the hanky out of my pocket and wipe the blood away, and I can see a pretty large piece of tree stuck in his head. I tell him that he has a piece of the tree in his head, and he grins and says, "Well, get it out."

I try to get ahold of it just as the next slug slams into the tree and bark splinters all around us and we both duck. I tell him to hold still, and I jerk the piece of wood out of his scalp. He is bleeding pretty badly so I wrap his head with my hanky. I say, "Buck, I am going to try and work back around and try and get a fix on the shooter. You send some fire the direction the shots are coming from while I make a break for it. If I can get to that ravine over there and you can draw their fire, I might be able to pick up a muzzle blast and pinpoint the shooter."

Buck says, "Okay, on three. One, two, three," and he starts shooting.

I make my break, and there is no return fire until Buck stops firing. I can see the muzzle flash about two hundred yards from Buck's location on a ridge behind and south of the garage. From my vantage point, I can see the reflection of a scope.

I stay still and wait on Buck to let loose another volley, and when he does, I start to move again. I am moving slowly along the inside of the ravine when I hear Buck rip off another volley. When he stops shooting, I hear the report of the rifle again. I pick up the pace. From where I am in the ravine now, I can't see the area where shooter is.

I keep moving as quickly as I can in the rough terrain. I am having a hard time keeping quiet and keeping my footing when suddenly I trip over a root, and I go tumbling down the inside of the ravine into the ditch at the bottom.

As I gather myself, I hear the motorcycle start up and gravel fly as it tears up the drive. I am furious with myself, and I mutter some not very gentlemanly words as I stand up, wet and muddy.

When I try to take a step, I realize I have cut my calf pretty badly, but I can walk. As I make my way up the hill, I can hear Buck hollering for me. I holler back, "I am okay!"

When I get up to the crest of the hill, Buck is waiting on me. His head is wrapped, and I am bleeding and limping. Buck looks at me and says, "Cass is going be proud of us."

I say, "It isn't going to be pretty, is it?"

He says, "Nope."

Buck says, "Do you have a cellphone, John?"

I say, "Yes, why?"

He says, "Because two of my tires were sliced."

"It just keeps getting better. Okay," I say, "Let's call Cass." I get my phone out and look at the screen. I have no signal.

Buck sees the screen on my phone, and he says, "Calm mind, all storms must pass."

I have to laugh at that because I know that is the truth, but I also know that when we get ahold of Cass, this is probably the calm before the storm. We start limping up the drive, waving the phone around looking for a signal. Darn my calf hurts, darn my pride hurts.

Buck says, "That was exhilarating."

I say, "I am not sure that those are the words I would have chosen."

Buck says, "How do the words *resounding failure* sound then?"

I say, "Okay, let's go with *exhilarating* then. We have a signal."

Buck says, "I am not calling her."

I say, "Okay, why don't we flip for it?"

Buck says, "She is your girlfriend."

I say, "She is not my girlfriend."

Buck says, "Maybe we should text her."

I laugh and say, "Great idea, what will the text say?"

Buck says, "Stranded, stop, need help, stop, sycamore road, old man, Tony's garage, stop."

I say, "Buck, we are not sending a telegram."

He says, "Then shut up and call her."

I dial the phone and put it up to my ear. It rings once, and I hear Cass's voice. "Where are you two?"

I start out with "I am sorry," and it goes downhill from there.

CHAPTER 36

The Storm Before the Calm

The Cass caravan gets to us about twenty minutes after we made the call. Cass and Dixie in the SUV, a tow truck, and a forensics team. Cass steps out of the SUV and looks at Buck and I and says, "I should be so mad at you two."

Buck starts to say something, and I say, "Buck, don't say it. Cass is right."

Buck says, "About what?"

I say, "Whatever she is going to say."

Buck thinks a moment and says, "Yeah, good idea."

Cass says, "What was the last thing I said to you two boys?"

We look at each other, and I say, "Something about not getting in trouble, I think."

Cass says, "Yes, something like that. So, tell me in detail what happened here."

Buck and I tell her the tale of our misadventure as best we can, all the while waiting for the storm to come. But instead she makes it even more uncomfortable for us by not letting us have it. When we finish, Cass says, "Did you go in the garage yet?"

I say, "No, we thought it would be best to wait on you."

Cass says, "It is way too late to try and curry favor with me."

Buck says, "I hate curry."

Cass says, "Not funny." I get caught grinning, and that was a mistake. Cass says, "Let's go take a look at that garage."

Buck and I follow quietly behind Cass, trying not to look at each other, afraid we will laugh. Cass says, "I can hear you two not talking back there."

We don't say anything, we just keep following her. When we reach the garage, Cass says, "Buck, you go around the building to the back. John, you follow me in."

Buck and I echo each other as we say, "Yes, sheriff."

Cass rolls her eyes at us and says, "Everwhat."

Buck asks, "What did she say?"

I say, "Go to the back, Buck."

Cass pulls her gun and so do Buck and I. She raps the door and hollers, "Police. Is anyone on there?" No answer so she pushes the door open and hollers again. Still no answer.

Gun up, she enters the garage with me close behind, and Buck works his way around the building. When we get inside, we see that the place is all torn apart. Someone was looking for something in here, there is no doubt. Cass takes a walk around the room, checks the back-office area, and hollers, "Clear."

Buck comes in the back door and Cass tells him to search the outside of the building and he steps back out. We do a thorough search of the inside and find nothing but a mess. When we go back out the front, we find Buck waiting on us. Cass asks me where the shooter was and tells the forensics team to process this scene and for us to wait SUV with Dixie.

When we get to the SUV, we start arguing about who will sit in front. Buck stops the argument by opening the back door and getting in with Dixie. Buck says, "Hi dog."

Dixie says, "Woof."

I say, "You two were made for each other," and Buck slams the door shut.

I get in the front seat, and we wait on Cass. When she finishes talking to her team, she walks back and gets in the SUV. She sits there a moment but does not start the vehicle. Finally, she says, "You two could have been killed."

Buck and I don't say anything. Cass says, "Don't you have anything to say?"

I say, "Sorry."

Cass says, "That's it. Sorry."

I say, "What else do you want us to say?"

"How about three little words?" she says.

I say, "I am sorry."

Buck laughs, and Cass goes off. She says, "No, these three—I am sorry Cass, we should never have gone to the garage without calling you to go with us. You are the sheriff, not us. We are retired and have no jurisdiction here. It was a stupid idea, please forgive us. Those three words!"

Buck says, "It was my idea."

Cass says, "did Rambo here try and change your mind?" Buck does not respond. Cass says, "Just as I thought. You two don't talk. I need to think." She starts the SUV and takes off.

When she pulls out of the driveway, Buck says, "The office is the other direction."

Cass says, "I told you to be quiet." We both look straight ahead and don't talk. Even Dixie is subdued. When she turns in the drive, I turn and look at Buck, but I don't say a word.

Cass does not say a thing until she stops and parks. She shuts the SUV off and says, "Get out."

We get out, and Buck whispers, "Where are we?"

I say, "You don't know?"

He says, "Not a clue."

I say, "Well, hold on and follow the sheriff," and let Dixie out.

CHAPTER 37

Life is Full of Surprises

Buck opens the door for Dixie as the door to the bungalow opens, and Dixie takes off at a dead run, tail up and eyes shining. She stops at the front door and sits until Joann steps out of the door.

Joann immediately bends to rub Dixies head, and even though I have already met her, I am still amazed at her simple yet elegant beauty. For a woman in her sixties, she is stunning. Not model pretty and not cover girl pretty, she is hair in the wind, barefoot on the beach, no makeup, sun on her face and a laugh on her lips pretty. The kind of pretty that makes you think to yourself, *I bet she got prettier as she aged.*

I look over at Buck and he is staring at Joann, unabashed. I don't think he even cares she is looking right back at him.

Cass speaks up and says, "I brought you two here to get you cleaned up."

Joann breaks the stare down by saying, "Hey, you guys look like you could use some TLC."

Cass says, "No, Mom, they need to be slapped."

Buck turns to Cass and says, "Mom?"

Cass says, "Yes, my mom."

Buck asks her, "Why did you not tell me she lived here?"

Cass says, "You did not ask."

Buck starts to respond, but I interrupt him and say, "Hi Joann. We are at your mercy, it would seem."

Joann says, "I told you that you were welcome in my home anytime, John, and that still stands."

I take a glance at Cass and catch her looking at me. She turns her head and starts toward the bungalow without speaking. Buck and I follow her sheepishly to the door.

Joann says to me, "You go to the mud room and undress. There is a robe there for you, John. Leave you dirty clothes on the table, and there is shower right around the corner to right." She says, "Now you, Buck, you come here and let me look at your head."

Buck steps up in front of her, and she says, "Bend down a little bit there, big man." Buck grins at her words and bends his head down to her.

Joann pulls at his blood-matted hair and says, "That wound bled pretty bad, I would guess, but I don't think you need stitches. Let's clean the cut up and wash the blood out of your hair and dress that wound."

Buck grins like a schoolboy, Cass glares at him, and I go straight to my strong suit—I do something stupid. I say, "You two would make a great couple."

Joann laughs, Buck turns red, Cass glares, and I just stand there. Joann says, "I think we all need to relax. It has been a trying day."

Cass says, "You have no idea, Mom."

The four of us go into the bungalow—me, Joann, Buck and Dixie—as Cass walks back to the SUV. I holler at her, "Where are you going?"

She says, "Away from you two," and she gets in and pulls away. I walk back up to the bungalow and go to the mud room and do as I was told.

When I get out of the shower, I find a pair of flip flops by the robe and a towel, so I dry off and put the robe on. I walk in to the kitchen to find Buck and Joann sitting at the table, drinking coffee and so deep in conversation they don't notice me come in.

I stand for a moment, watching them and listening when Joann says, "John, come join us. Coffee is on the counter, and the cups are right above."

I say thank you and get myself a cup of coffee. I walk over and sit down just in time to hear Buck quote C.S. Lewis, "You know when Penny died, I remembered what C.S. Lewis said about grief. 'No one ever told me that grief felt so like fear.'"

Joann has tears in her eyes as she responds, "That is exactly how I felt when Bill was killed."

I sit down quietly and decide this is a good time for me to stay that way. They continue to talk like old friends as I quietly sip my coffee. Finally, Joann notices me again and says, "I just heard the washer shut off. I will get your clothes in the dryer, John."

I stop her as she starts to get up and say, "No, please allow me. You have done enough already."

I get up and go back to the mud room and put the clothes in the dryer and go back to the kitchen. I find Buck and Joann still deep in conversation. I decide to go out on the porch, and Dixie decides she is bored with the conversation and follows me outside. I take a seat on the porch swing, and Dixie jumps up beside me.

It is a little chilly with the breeze off of the ocean, but it also feels a little like home. I lean back, take a sip of my coffee, and close my eyes as Dixie lays her head on my lap. The Eagles song "Peaceful Easy Feeling" starts to play on the phonograph in my mind, and I hear Cass pull up.

I open my eyes as she gets out of the SUV and heads toward me. She says, "Get dressed. We need to talk."

CHAPTER 38

Guns and Roses

Cass is waiting on the porch when I come back dressed in my slightly damp clothes. She says, "Have a seat, John."

I sit down and wait on her to talk. She has a cup of coffee in her hands and starts out by saying, "My mom and Buck are in their own little world in there." She looks at me, but I don't respond. I just sit there in silence waiting on Cass to say something, but she is just kind of staring off at the sea now.

Finally, I speak, "Cass, are you okay?"

She breaks her stare at the sea and turns to me and says, "No. You come here to my quiet little county and now my whole world is upside down. I was in a nice groove here. I knew pretty much what each day would hold. I went to work, and I went back to my boring but quiet home. I visited my mom once a week, and no one knew anything about me. I was a very private person in a very public job."

I decide I should still not talk so I don't. Cass looks at me again and stands up, steps in front of me and says, "Darn it, John, I really like you, and I care a lot about Buck. You two put a scare in me today, and I am feeling things that I don't know what to do with. You could have been killed."

Now I speak. "But we weren't. We are scratched up but okay. Cass, Buck and I may be retired, but we are still cops. We should not have went to the garage without telling you, and for that, I am sorry. So, Cass, please forgive me."

Cass says, "Those three words will work, but don't you dare do anything like that again!"

I say, "I promise you."

She sits back down and says, "Okay, let's talk about this case." She says, "The prints are back on the shell casings from the shooter at the garage. It was a 30-30, and the prints belong to a Butch Wagner from West Virginia. He is a member of the Skulls biker gang we visited and has a rather long rap sheet. He has a reputation as a strong-arm enforcer and has numerous assault charges on his sheet.

"It would appear to me that he was looking for something or someone or both, and you interrupted his search. I think that B4 has lost track of Joseph also. If you came before whoever was storing guns in your barn expected you too, I am guessing you messed up a shipment or interrupted one."

I say, "I agree." I ask, "What is our next move?"

She says, "We really need to find Joseph or this Butch Wagner." I ask her where we go to next, and she says, "I am not sure."

At that moment, Buck and Joann walk out onto the porch, Joann with her arm through Bucks'.

I don't want to look at Cass, but I can't help myself. I turn toward her, and she looks at me like, "What the heck is going on here?" I turn away quickly and do it again—I say something stupid. "Don't you two make a nice-looking couple?"

Cass says, "Buck, I need your help here. Can you let go of my mom and help me?"

Joann says, "Cass, now you need to be nice young lady. Buck and I have had a wonderful visit." Then she says, "I will go back inside while you three talk business out here. And Buck, I will see you Friday night."

Cass says, "Where do you think we should go next to look for Joseph, and what does my mom mean I will see you Friday night?"

"Okay," Buck says. "First question, there is a place down on the docks we should go next, and second question, your mom and I are going to a fundraiser for the homeless shelter Friday night."

Cass is speechless, I believe, and I am trying not to smile. Buck is oblivious to both of us and obviously smitten. Now this is an unforeseen turn of events. I think to myself, *Wow, I should have come here sooner. I am really having a good time.*

I look at Cass, and I am relatively sure she is not having a good time at this moment. Buck asks Cass, "Does your mom like roses?"

Cass says, "Really, Buck, I am only interested in guns right now, and she likes sunflowers and daisies."

CHAPTER 39

Don't Dock My Pay

The four of us go back inside to say our goodbyes and thank you to Joann before we leave. Dixie is first in line for her head rub and a doggy hug, then I take my turn, and I get a hug and a whisper to be extra nice to Cass, then Buck steps up, and Joann takes his hands in hers and gives him the sweetest little peck on the cheek and a wink as she releases him.

Now it is Cass's turn. As she steps up to her mom, she seems a little unsure of herself, and Joann says, "Cass, life is full of changes honey, you know that."

Buck says, "If I may quote C.S. Lewis, 'You can't go back and change the beginning, but you can start where you are and change the ending.'"

Joann says, "Well, aren't you the fountain of wisdom, Buck?"

Buck blushes, I laugh, and Cass grimaces as she says, "That does not mean I have to like it."

I say, "Okay, it is my turn. My grandpa said, 'If you are afraid of change, you should only carry paper money,'" to which Cass replies, "That is the stupidest thing I have ever heard."

I ask, "Are you calling my grandpa stupid?"

Cass says, "No, I am calling you stupid."

Joann says, "How sweet, your first lovers quarrel."

Cass turns, and as she is stomping out, she does not turn back as she says, "You three get in the SUV, and Mom, I will deal with you later."

Buck, Dixie, and I all look to Joann for help, and she just shrugs and says, "You all better get moving, or she will leave without you."

I wave, Buck grins, and Dixie barks and off to the SUV we go. As we make the drive to the docks in silence, I think about a line from a Nicholas Sparks book made into a movie *The Choice*.

In it, the lead male character Travis says to the lead female Gabby, "You bother me." It was their way of saying "No one else makes me feel like you do, and I love you" playfully and unique to their relationship. I kind of think of Cass and I, and I realize that she bothers me too. I have never felt like this and I don't think she has either and we don't know what to do with it.

I break the silence by saying to Cass, "You bother me."

She gives me a quick grin and says, "Yeah, you bother me too, John." That brings a smile to my face, and I am fine with the silence.

Buck says, "Okay, right up here on the left, you will see the sign for Sunset Pier, turn in, and stay to the water side where the road splits."

Cass says, "Okay, what are we looking for?"

Buck says, "There is a little bar up here right next to the Dive Shop called Cindy's Dive Bar. She owns both places."

I say, "I can't wait to meet her."

Buck says, "She is unique. John," which leads me to ask "Hey, do you know how to catch a unique rabbit?"

Buck says, "I don't know."

I say, "Unique up on it."

Buck laughs, and Cass says, "There is something wrong with both of you," but I see the grin on her face as she turns in to the Dive Bar.

We park, and Cass says, "I think we should leave Dixie in the SUV."

I say, "Okay, but let's leave the windows down for her. She won't jump out."

Cass agrees, rolls down the windows, and I tell Dixie to stay. She lays down in the backseat, and we head toward the bar. Cass tells Buck to go around back and make sure no one tries to leave.

Cass and I go to the front door and take a look around. We both spot the motorcycle besides the building, and we unsnap our guns as we go in cautiously.

Upon entering, I see why Buck called Cindy unique. Cindy is a tiny oriental woman with facial tattoos and spiked pink-and-purple hair. She is pretty but hard. When she sees Cass and me, she says, "Five-O." *A little bit on the loud side,* I think to myself.

I catch her eyes, take a quick glance toward the doorway to her right that goes, I assume, into the back room or kitchen. I hear the backdoor slam, and then I hear the crack of a gunshot.

Cass tells Cindy not to move and for me to stay here. She runs around the bar and through the doorway into the back room. I hear the door slam again and then nothing.

At this point, I have my own gun out, and I have it trained on Cindy. I tell her to keep her hands where I can see them. Cindy does not speak, and she does not move. We wait a few minutes, and I hear the back door again. I move my aim toward the doorway and watch the entrance. The first one through the doorway is Buck, and he is followed by Cass and a man in handcuffs.

I ask Buck, "Who fired the shot?" and Buck says, "He needed a reason to stop running so I reminded him I have a gun."

I ask, "Is this Butch?"

Buck says, "He is not talking, but we think he is Butch."

Cass says, "We will know very shortly," as she walks him over to a chair and tells him to sit. He sits, and Cass tells Buck to keep an eye on him. Cass walks over to the bar and says to Cindy, "You have a little explaining to do here."

Cindy says, "What do you mean?"

Cass points at the handcuffed guy and asks her, "Who is this guy?"

She says, "I have never seen him before today."

Cass asks, "Then why was he in your back room?"

Cindy does not flinch when she says, "Hey, he saw you guys coming and went by me out the back."

I say, "So when you said Five-O really loud, that was not a signal."

She says, "I don't know what you are talking about."

Cass turns to the other patrons and asks loudly, "Do any of you know this man?" and points at the handcuffed guy. No one responds. Cass says to Cindy, "It looks like you will be coming with us back to the station."

Cindy asks, "On what charge?"

"Harboring a fugitive," Cass says. Just then a deputy walks into the bar. Cass points to the prisoner and says to the deputy, "Take this gentleman back to the station and lock him up. No phone call for him until I get back."

Cass tells everyone to leave and waits until they are all out of the door, and she says to Cindy, "Okay, last chance to talk before we haul you in."

She looks around the room, and sighs as she says, "What do you want to know?"

CHAPTER 40

The Information Highway

When Cass gets done talking to Cindy, she tells her, "Don't leave town in case we need to talk to you again."

She says, "I'm not going anywhere. Everything I own is here."

Cass says, "If you stay involved with people like this, you won't own anything, you will be in prison."

Cindy lowers her head and starts wiping the bar down. We all walk out to the SUV and load up to go to the station. On the way, we go over what Cindy told us. It was not a lot of information, but we believe it was all she knew.

She told us that Butch had been in before with Joseph in the past, but this time he had come in looking for Joseph. When Cindy asked him why he was looking for Joseph, he said that his boss thought Joseph had something that did not belong to him.

Cindy said that last night Butch was very drunk and said something about guns being stolen, then he clammed up, said not to repeat it. She said she told him about the old garage up the coast, and he told her he was doing to go out there today. She said that she asked Butch who he worked for, but he told her he could not tell her, but it was someone local and someone important. That was all we had but it told us we were on the right track.

When we get back to the station, Cass says, "I will interrogate Butch, and you two can listen in." When we pull up to the station, I tell Cass to go on in, and Buck and I will be in a little bit. She looks at me and says, "Don't be long."

Buck and I let Dixie out to do her business, and we sit down on the bench outside the station. I look at Buck and he looks at me and we both start laughing.

Buck says, "Heck of a day."

I say, "Yeah, heck of a day."

Buck and I sit and watch Dixie sniffing around, and she comes over to me and sits down, looking for a petting. I oblige her and so does Buck.

Buck says, "I think I remember seeing a dog like this with Joseph."

I say, "This is probably her." I give him the short version of how I found her, and he agrees that it very well could be the same dog.

When I tell him how she responded at Joseph's house, he says, "Yep, this must be her."

I ask him, "So what's up with Joann?"

He says, "She is quite a woman, John."

I answer, "I noticed that myself."

Buck grins and says, "I have not met anyone since Penny passed that even stirred any interest in me."

I grin and say, "There must be something about the women in that family."

Buck says, "Yeah, I noticed."

We both laugh a bit as we share a couple of old stories, and then Cass comes to the door and says, "If you two are done lying to each other, come on in here."

We put Dixie in the SUV and head on in to the station. When we get inside, Cass calls us in to her office and says, "He lawyered up on us. We are not going to get anything out of him. His attorney is on the way in. I talked to the prosecutor, and we definitely have enough to hold him." Cass says, "I want his boss, and we can't tie him to the body on the beach so maybe we can cut a deal and get to the big man."

Buck and I agree with her, and she says, "His attorney will be here in about an hour." Cass says, "You two are quite a duo."

I say, "Yeah, like Starsky and Hutch." And Buck says, "Maybe Turner and Hooch."

I say, "You can't be Hooch, I already have a dog."

Cass stops, says, "Enough already. Having you two around is like having two kids."

I say, "You didn't tell me you have kids. Buck, did you know she has kids?"

Buck laughs, and Cass says, "You guys never stop."

I say, "Okay, seriously, sheriff, what's our next move?"

Cass says, "I am hungry. Let's grab lunch."

I look at Buck and say, "You guys have really interesting restaurant names here." I wonder where we are going.

Cass hears me and says, "Dairy Sweet. We are in a hurry." She says to a deputy, "We are leaving his dog here. Be nice to her."

The deputy grimaces but says, "Yes ma'am, I will. Do you want me to cage her with our other dogs?"

Cass looks at me first, then at the deputy, and says, "No, she will be fine I here. She has better manners then both of these two," and points at me and Buck.

I point out some of the major differences between Dixie and I, but Cass is already walking away. When we get outside, I can see the Dairy Sweet down the street, and since Cass keeps walking, Buck and I follow her.

When we get to the Dairy Sweet, I hold the door for Cass, and we walk up to the counter to place our orders. I say, "Ladies first," so Cass places her order, points at me, and tells the girl, "He is paying."

I tell Buck, "I got yours too," and we both order and sit with Cass. While we wait for our food and sip our drinks, we talk over the events of the day. The conversation is light as we all need a break from the investigation. Our food arrives, and we eat an uneventful meal.

When we are finished, Cass says, "I am proud of you two—no guns, no punching, and no bad jokes. Are you guys okay?"

Neither of us think it is a good time to answer, so we don't. We head back to the station, and as we are walking, we see a black Mercedes pulls up to in front of it. A man in an Armani suit gets out, and Buck says, "He really looks important."

Cass says, "Well, what do you say we go show him some country hospitality, boys?"

Buck and I smile, and I say, "This should be fun."
Cass says, "I get worried when you say that."
Buck says, "You should."

CHAPTER 41

Put Out the Welcome Mat

Mr. Armani goes up the steps and into the front door of the station, and Cass, Buck, and I follow him. I can't help myself as I say, "Every girl crazy 'bout a sharp-dressed man."

Buck says, "All we need now are some cheap sunglasses."

Cass asks, "Do I need to remind you two how serious this is?"

Buck says, "Probably."

When we get inside, we see Armani at the front desk talking to a deputy. The deputy spots us and says, "Great timing, sir. This is the sheriff."

Armani turns around to face us and says, "My name is Mason Cantrell. I am Mr. Wagner's attorney."

Cass says, "And I am Sheriff Quince."

Cantrell looks at me and Buck and asks Cass, "And who are these two intriguing gentlemen?"

I say, "Well, let me introduce us to you. I am retired Sheriff John Young, and this is retired Sheriff Buck Branson."

Armani looks us over and says, "Is this a police station or a retirement home?"

I suggest that unless his suit is body armor, he should shut up.

Buck laughs and says, "And he has a nasty right cross."

Armani collects himself and steps away from me and says to Cass, "I don't have time to play with your senior citizens so let's get down to it concerning my client."

Cass tells him to step into her office as he says, "I need to see the crime scene report." Cass tells the deputy to bring it to her office, and she tells me and Buck we can only come if we don't speak.

Buck says he would rather spend time with Dixie than him, but I say, "I wouldn't miss this for anything."

When we get in her office Armani asks, "Who is Dixie?"

Cass nonchalantly says, "A dog."

Armani does not respond to it but says, "Give me a moment to read the report please."

Cass and I wait patiently while he reads it. He lays it down and asks, "Do you want to release him now or in the morning when the Judge tells you to?"

Cass says, "We have his prints on at least six casings, and he fired on two cops and left the scene."

Armani gets a really smug look on his face and says, "Who said my client fired first?"

Cass says, "Both witnesses."

Armani asks, "Who were the witnesses again?"

Cass says, "You know who they were."

Armani says, "Refresh my memory please."

Cass says, "Sheriffs Young and Branson."

"Didn't I hear them introduce themselves as retired?" he asked.

"Yes, you did," I say.

Cass says, "John, you are supposed to be observing."

I don't say anything, but Armani smiles and says, "Okay, Sheriff let me see if I have this right. You have two retired, not active officers who were trespassing, that say my client fired at them first."

Cass says, "That is one way of looking at it."

Armani says, "That is the way I will present it to the judge. I will have no trouble getting bail for him, and if it gets anywhere near going to court, you will have a hard time winning this one, sheriff."

Cass says, "That is possible, but after you talk to your client, he will be sleeping here tonight."

Armani says, "Take me to my client."

Cass says, "One more thing, who do you work for, Mr. Cantrell?"

Armani says, "Why, my client, sheriff."

Cass says, "That guy in there can't afford your shoes."

Armani laughs and says, "You noticed. Thank you, they are Berluti Scritto custom-made. A man's shoes say a lot about him.

"So does the clients he represents," Cass says.

Armani glares at Cass and says, "Take me to my client now."

Cass takes him to the lawyer-client meeting room and says, "The prisoner will be right in a little while."

I can hear Armani yelling he does not like to wait as Cass slams the door. Cass tells the deputy "Give him 15 minutes before you take his client in." Cass says, "Let's go to my office and talk, and go get Buck in here."

I say, "Yes ma'am," and head out to get Buck. When I get outside, I see that Buck has company. Mrs. Braun is petting Dixie and talking to Buck.

I walk up to them, and she looks at me and says, "I heard you guys had a little excitement out to old man Miller's garage."

I ask, "How did you hear that?"

She says, "Now John, it's a small town."

I tell Buck that the sheriff wants us to come in, and we excuse ourselves from Patty. As we walk away, she says, "I saw Joseph today."

We both turn and say, "Where?"

She says, "I saw him down by the docks early today when I went to our boat. I don't think he saw me, and he seemed in a hurry."

I tell her, "Thanks for the heads up," and Buck and I go back to the station. When we get inside, I tell Cass "we just got some interesting news."

She says, "Good or bad? I could use some good news right now."

I say, "Good and bad."

Cass says, "Beats all bad, I guess. Tell me what you got."

Buck and I sit down and share the new info with Cass. Through her window, we see Armani leave, talking on his cellphone.

Cass says, "I would love to know who is on the other end of that call."

Buck and I don't say anything, but the wheels are turning.

CHAPTER 42

Who Knew

Cass says, "I need to think for a moment."

Buck and I decide to take a walk, so we excuse ourselves, and I tell Cass, "We are going to get some fresh air and let you think." She nods her head and waves us off.

Buck and I get Dixie and head outside. I ask Buck, "Did you get them?"

He says, "Yes," and he hands me the keys to Cass's SUV.

I say, "Let's go then." I say, "There is only one motel in town, right?"

Buck says, "Yep, the Wave Runner." Buck says, "hey, do you remember Jason?"

I say, "Yeah, Buck, I remember."

Buck laughs and says, "I bet it would be a different result now."

I say, "Probably, but you never know in a fight, and you taught me that you only fight to stop something worse than the actual fight for protection of yourself or someone else and never just to prove you are tougher than the other guy."

Buck says, "So I taught you that. I am pretty smart."

I say, "Most of the time. Just not recently."

He laughs and says, "I am on a roll."

I grin and say, "I am not faring much better, my friend."

Buck says, "There is some consolation in that."

I had forgotten how much I enjoyed our verbal sparring. It reminded me of Cass and me talking over the last day and a half.

It does not take us but a few minutes to get to the motel, and we find what we are looking for right away. The black Mercedes is in the parking lot, and surprise, there is a black Navigator there also. I look over at Buck and say, "This motel sure draws some high-class guests."

Buck says, "Yeah, I heard you stayed here."

I laugh as Buck says, "It looks like the clientele went downhill since you stayed here."

I say, "Let's go back to the station before Cass realizes we took her car."

On the way back to the station, we discuss that it looks as though everyone involved here is working for Sly. When we pull up in front of the station, we find Cass standing on the front steps. She comes right down to the SUV and says, "What is wrong with you two?"

Before I can speak, Buck says, "It was my idea, Cass. All we did was to go by the motel and see if Armani was staying there."

She says, "And?"

"Yes, he is, and guess who was there also?" Cass doesn't say anything, she just looks at Buck. Buck gives in first and says, "A black Navigator."

Cass says, "B4?"

I answer, "It was his vehicle."

Cass says, "Did you approach them?"

We say "no" at the same time. Cass looks us both up and down and says, "Okay guys, I want your undivided attention. Read my lips as I explain how this will work. I am the sheriff, you are not. I am an elected officer of the law with the authority to arrest and interrogate suspects. You are not. I am in charge here. You are not. I will make all the decisions on where we go and what we do. You will not. You two will go to crime scenes with me when I ask you to. Is that clear to you?"

Buck and I just stand there. It was so quiet you could hear a heart break or a tear drop. Cass says, "Let me ask you again, is that clear to you?"

I answer, "Yes, sheriff."

Buck says, "Yes, sheriff."

Cass says, "Good, now let's go back into my office and go over the information we have."

We both say nothing because, well, we both have nothing to say.

CHAPTER 43

Let's Talk

Buck and I take our seats across from Cass, and we do it quietly. Cass sits down and ruffles through some papers on her desk as we hold our peace. When she is done shuffling papers, she looks up at us. "You two are being awful quiet."

We just sit there. Buck breaks the silence when he says, "We are both not very good at following, so please forgive us, Cass."

I say, "Yes, we agree you are in charge, this is your county, and your case. How can we help you?"

Cass says, "Why thank you, Mr. Erp."

I laugh and say, "You can call me Wyatt, ma'am."

The tension is starting to break, and when Buck says, "I want to be Doc Holiday," it is enough to get us all three laughing.

As we go over all of the evidence we have to this point, Cass starts a bulletin board of events and suspects. When we finish up, Sly is at the top of it. I say, "I don't know if Sly is smart enough to be the mastermind here."

Buck says, "But there isn't anyone else in this cluster that could be the boss."

I say, "I agree with you, but I just don't think he has it in him. I know he comes from a long line of shysters, I mean Brauns, but he is just not that sharp."

Cass says, "I agree with you, John. B4 does not have the courage and the wherewithal to handle brokering guns. That is a dog-eat-dog business, and it involves really bad people. People that would eat Sly alive."

Buck says, "You are probably right, but how do we get the big boss to show up?"

We all sit in silence as we ponder the question. Cass says we have to bring some kind of pressure to bare to get someone to make a mistake. I say, "I think that we can get Sly to panic and make a mistake."

Buck says, "Yeah, that attorney seems like he has been around the block a few times. I doubt that he will flinch." Cass and I agree with that sentiment, and we all go back to silent running.

Cass says, "I have an idea." We both lean forward as Cass spells out what she has in mind. We agree that it might work, and at the very least, it will make him mad. We have some details to work out when Bucks phone rings.

He answers, "Hello, this is Buck." Cass and I stop talking so he can hear. Well, maybe so we can hear. Buck has a smile on his face as he listens, but he does not say anything that would give away who he is talking to. I look at the smile in his eyes, and I know who it is.

When he hangs up he asks, "Do you guys need me anymore tonight?"

Cass says, "No, I think that John and I can navigate this next step alone."

He gets up to go and says, "Call me if you need me."

Cass says, "Wait a minute, you can't just leave like that without telling us where you are going."

He says, "Yep, I sure can." And off he goes. He turns back around and asks, "Can one of the deputies take me to get my truck?"

Cass says, "Only if you tell us where you are going."

Buck says, "Okay, I will walk."

Cass says, "Darn it, Buck, John can take you while I catch up here."

She tosses me the keys, and I tell her I will be back in little while. I say, "Let's go Buck, Dixie is probably wondering where the heck I am."

As we go out the front door, I say, "Are you sure you want to go down this road, Buck?"

He says, "Oh yeah, I am very sure."

I laugh and say, "Okay, let's get your truck."

When I finish delivering Buck to his truck, and we say our goodnights, I head back to Cass. When Dixie and I get back to the station, Cass is waiting on us. Her office door is open, so we go on in. Dixie runs over to Cass for her petting, and I take a seat across from her.

As she is petting Dixie without looking up, she says, "It took a minute to sink in. I guess I was distracted. Buck is with my mom."

I say, "Yes."

She looks up at me and says, "What the heck, John, they just met."

Tongue in cheek, I say, "Crazy, huh, two people meet and instant chemistry. Makes no sense."

Cass starts to say something but stops, looks at me, and starts laughing.

I say, "This has been a crazy two days."

Cass says, "Crazy just barely covers it, cowboy, and this day is not over yet."

I ask "Did you talk to the judge?"

She says, "Yes, it was a hard sell, but I got it."

I say, "What are we waiting on? This is gonna be fun."

Cass says, "I always get nervous when you say that."

I say, "You should. Let's go."

CHAPTER 44

Under Pressure

Cass, Dixie, and I load back into the SUV, and we head out. Cass says, "I bet they don't see this coming, and I agree that this will be a surprise."

As we make our way along the coast, Cass and I talk about all the evidence we have collected so far. It has been a very interesting two days up to this point. What we have right now is all speculation but based on a series of events that would lead us to some specific conclusions. We know who some of the players are at this point, but we don't really have any idea who is the big boss is.

Up on the right, I see the sign for the Sunset Pier again. Cass turns on her turn light and makes the turn toward the pier area one more time. As we make our way down the drive, Cass says, "We were fortunate that B4's buddy Judge Clifton was out of town. We would not have gotten the search warrant for the boat if Clifton would have been here."

Cass slows down as she sees the sign for slip number 16. When we pull in, I see there is a R-8 Audi Ice silver convertible setting there. I tell Cass, "That ain't no Ford," and she laughs and says, "Yeah I know, that is Patty's car."

I say to Cass "This is even better. We can question her while we are searching the boat."

As Cass and I get out of the SUV, we see Patty on the upper deck get up from her lawn chair and wave at us. I don't spend much time looking at Patty because I am looking at the boat. It is a beautiful 1989 Buddy Davis sportfish. I'm thinking to myself, *This is about* *a $290,000 boat. How in the world can B4 afford this baby, not to mention the Audi R-8 I see parked here?*

I ask Cass, "Did you know they owned a boat like this?"

She answers me, "I had no idea, John. It would appear there is a lot about the Braun family that I didn't know."

I say to Cass, "You really had no reason to look at him. It would appear this was all happening quietly and without any casualties up to this point. They had quite the little deal going on."

Cass yells up at Patty and tells her to come on down and that we need to talk to her. Patty yells, "I will be right down!"

Cass yells back, "And put something on over that swimsuit please!"

Patty laughs and slips on a white see-through, sheer swimsuit cover up that looks like it is from Victoria's Secret. Cass just shakes her head, looks at me, and says, "What are you looking at?"

I say, "A suspect. She might have a gun hidden under that bikini."

Cass laughs and says, "She couldn't hide a piece of candy in that bathing suit."

I say, "Should we search her?"

Cass says, "If you want to be tased, sure."

I say, "My, aren't we touchy today."

Cass says, "Maybe I will tase you just for fun."

I say, "That would be police brutality," and Cass says, "Anyone who knows you would say it was justified."

I grin and say, "Okay, probably true."

At that moment Patty gets down to the lower level of the boat and purrs, "How can I help you, John?"

Cass says, "You can help me, Mrs. Braun," and hands her the warrant.

Patty looks it over, looks at me, and asks, "What is this about?"

Cass says, "It is a warrant to search this boat, and he is not the sheriff here, I am."

Patty says, "I don't know what Sylvester would say."

Cass says, "It does not matter what he would say, we have a warrant."

Patty says, "Okay then, I guess you should come aboard."

Cass and I step onto the boat, and Cass says, "You take the upper level, and I will take the hold."

I say, "Okay," and as I head for the steps, Patty follows me. I turn to her and say, "You should wait down with her on the deck."

She says, "It is my boat I will go where I want to."

I say, "Suit yourself," but I think to myself, *This will be a good opportunity to question her.*

When we get up top, she sits back down in her lawn chair and takes off the bathing suit cover and lays back in the chair. I have to admit she is beautiful, but I have no interest in her. My heart is not my own, and she is married and to a dirt bag. She asks me, "What are you guys looking for?"

I say, "Evidence."

She asks, "Of what?"

I say, "A crime."

She says, "What crime?"

I say, "Why don't you just let me do my search, Patty?"

She says, "Well, excuse me, Mr. Bigshot."

I laugh and say, "Okay, take it easy, Patty. Let's start over."

I see her visibly relax, and I make my move. I ask, "So do you and Sly go out on this baby a lot?"

She answers, "We hardly ever go out together, and I mostly just come here to tan and to get away from home."

I laugh and say, "This is an awful nice boat to just use it for a tanning bed."

As I continue my search, she keeps talking. She says, "Sylvester takes it up the coast about once a month to New York."

I ask, "What does he go up there for?"

"He says it is for his business, but I wonder if he has a girlfriend."

I say, "With a woman like you, why would he have a girlfriend?"

Patty says, "Thank you, John. You always were a gentleman."

I say, "You are too kind, Patty." I say, "Hey, does anyone go with him on these trips to New York?"

She says, "Yes, I think Joseph and one other guy sometimes."

I say, "Really, who is that?"

She says, "I don't know." She says, "Because he sometimes tells Cindy to pack for three when she gets the boat ready."

I say, "Who is Cindy?"

She answers, "The girl that owns the dive shop and bar down the beach." I don't respond to her, and she asks, "Do you know her?"

I say, "We just recently met." I feel someone watching me, and I turn and see Cass standing at the top of the stairs.

She says, "I hate to interrupt this reunion, but I think you should come down here, John."

I follow her down the stairs and into the hold. She points to a cushion and says, "What does that look like to you, John?" It looks like a blood stain. "I found it when I flipped it over to look underneath the seat. Tell Mrs. Braun to get off the boat immediately and go home. I am calling the forensics team in to scour this boat."

I go up and tell Patty she must leave, and after some complaining, she agrees to go when I tell her we will arrest her if she does not leave. I walk her off, and she leaves in a shower of gravel. I go back onto the boat and find Cass sitting on the lawn chair, deep in thought.

I don't interrupt, and I wait for her to acknowledge me. Finally, she turns to me and says, "I think this will be a book when it is over, John."

I can only smile as I say, "I wonder who the hero will be?"

CHAPTER 45

The Plot Thickens

We wait for about fifteen minutes, and the forensics team shows up. Right behind them slides in the black Navigator. We can't see through the tinted windows, but we know who it is.

Sly gets out of the vehicle, and he is spitting nails. I look at Cass, smile, and before I can say it, she says, "This is gonna be fun."

I look at her and say, "It makes me nervous when you say that."

She grins and says, "It should."

Sly storms up to the boat where a deputy stops him from boarding and says. "This is a possible crime scene, and you cannot come aboard, sir."

Sly lets loose a string of obscenities as Cass and I come down from the upper deck to talk to him. Sly's face is as red as a beet when we get to him. Sly says, "What the heck, sheriff? This is ridiculous. I am an upstanding citizen in this town."

Cass says, "You only got part of that right, Mr. Braun. You are a citizen of this town. Upstanding, probably not." Sly is steaming, and I am grinning. Cass says to Sly, "We need to ask you some questions, Mr. Braun."

He says, "Like what?"

"Like where did the blood come from on the pillow in the hull? Stuff like that."

Sly says, "I cut myself down there."

Cass says, "Then we will need a DNA sample from you to prove that it is your blood."

Before he can answer, another car comes flying up. The driver jumps out of the black Audi and says, "Don't answer any more questions, Mr. Braun."

Cass and I look at each other and grin. "This is great." Mason Cantrell to the rescue.

Sly turns to Mason and says, "This is crap. She wants me to give them a DNA sample."

Mason ignores him and says to Cass, "Sheriff Quince, my client will not be speaking to you here or any other time without me present. I am his attorney, and all questioning will be done in my presence."

Cass looks at Sly and asks, "Is that correct, Mr. Braun?"

He stutters a bit but says, "Yes."

Cass says to Cantrell, "We have your number at the station, and I will be calling you as soon as our team is done processing the evidence. Tell your client not to leave town."

Cantrell turns to Sly and says, "Let's go back to the dealership and talk, Mr. Braun."

As they walk away from us, I yell, "How did you two meet, anyway?"

Sly stops and starts to turn, but Cantrell grabs his arm and says, "Keep moving."

I yell after them, "You two were made for each other—a matched set." As they get into their respective cars, I turn to Cass and say, "You were right, that was fun."

Cass says, "It looks like we have accomplished what we were hoping to."

I agree with her. "There is no doubt that the pressure is starting to get to the players on the other team." I add, "And we may have evidence that the body on the beach was transported in Sly's boat."

Cass says, "Wouldn't that be special?"

I say, "*Special* will not be the word that Sly or Cantrell use."

Cass laughs and says, "That is for sure." She adds, "I have learned something important in this job, John."

I ask her, "And what would that be, sheriff?"

She grins and says, "Sometimes slime comes disguised as frosting, but when you look close, it is still slime."

161

I say, "You can't tell a foot by its shoe."

Cass says, "You just couldn't let me get in the last anecdote, could you, John?"

I say, "Madam, the floor is yours."

Cass thinks for a moment and says, "So the plot thickens."

I say, "Is that all you got?"

"Oh no, my dear Watson," she says. "You know my method. It is founded upon the observation of trifles."

I say, "Sherlock, you are amazing."

Cass laughs and says, "There is nothing more deceptive than an obvious fact."

I give her a bow and say, "I concede, I have seen too much not to know that the impression of a woman may be more valuable than the conclusion of an analytical reasoner."

She slaps at my arm and says, "That is exactly what I meant." Just then her phone rings, she looks at the number and says, "Just a minute, this could be important." She is animated as she talks to the person on the other end of the call.

When she hangs up, I ask her, "Who was it?"

She says, "That was Cleland."

CHAPTER 46

Guns and Rose

Cass tells the team that we have to leave and to finish up here and call her with any new results or news. We hurry out to the SUV, and as we load up, Dixie sits up and yawns. I say to her, "Are we boring you, girl?"

Dixie does respond—well, not with words, just a short woof. As we make our way back up the coast, I ask Cass, "What's going on?"

She says, "Cleland said to meet him the Rose's Roadhouse."

I ask her, "What kind of place is Rose's?"

She says, "After Rose retired from her first job, she opened a diner that caters to truck drivers, and let's call them the rougher crowd."

I ask, "What job did Rose retire from?"

Cass says, "She was a stripper."

I ponder that answer for a moment and decide not to respond. Cass looks over at me and says, "Good, no response, John."

I say, "See, I can be trained."

Cass says, "Dixie is more trainable than you, cowboy."

I laugh and say, "Why would you say that?"

Cass says, "Isn't it obvious? She is more intelligent." I laugh again and decide to let her have this one. She says, "Now don't hold back on me, John."

I say, "Sometimes discretion is the better part of valor."

Cass says, "Maybe you do have potential."

I say, "I have been fooling people for years."

Cass laughs, and her laughter is music in my ears. It has been a long day already, even though it is far from over, and it seems that Cass and I have lost some of the rhythm we had earlier.

When I think about the large number of events that have been crammed into the last two days, it is overwhelming. I guess it is a miracle that we have connected like we have in such a short time. Cass breaks up my reminiscing by saying, "We are here."

I look up and see the sign for Rose's Roadhouse as we turn in. Cleland is standing out front, smoking a cigarette when we pull in. Cass and I get out, and Cleland says quietly to Cass, "Act like you are rousting me."

Cass starts to holler at Cleland, and Cleland starts to holler back at Cass. Cass yells at him, "Unless you have an alibi, I am taking you in!"

Cleland says, "This is harassment."

Cass yells back, "Yes, it is." She tells him to put his hands behind his back and handcuffs him.

I say, "You shouldn't make her mad, Cleland. you know she will taser you in a heartbeat."

Cleland says, "That is not funny. She has tased me before. It hurts."

I say, "She threatens me all the time."

Cass says, "If you two are done reminiscing, let's get Cleland in the SUV."

We walk Cleland over to the vehicle, and when I open the back door, he sees Dixie and stops. He says, "I have seen that dog before."

Cass asks him, "Where?"

He says, "With Joseph. He treated that dog terrible. Does it bite?"

I grin and say, "I hope so. Now get in."

Cleland says, "That is not funny," but he gets in the backseat.

Cass and I get in and Cass starts the SUV and we take off. We go a mile or so, and Cass turns on a dirt road and goes around a corner behind the woods and pulls over. We get out of the SUV and let Cleland out of the backseat.

Cass says, "Turn around so I can uncuff you." He does, and Cass takes off the cuffs.

Cleland rubs his wrists and says, "Kind of tight there, sheriff."

Cass says, "Quit whining and tell me what you have."

Cleland looks at me and says, "Man, she is touchy today."

I say, "if I was you, I would start talking."

Cleland says, "Everybody is touchy today." Cass just glares at him, and Cleland says, "Okay, this is what I heard. There is a local business man who has been shipping guns up to New York and bringing something back here."

Cass and I look at each other but don't say anything. Cleland says, "Whatever is coming back is being kept under tight wraps. No one seems to have any idea what it is."

Cass says, "It seems odd that something is coming back, and it just disappears."

Cleland says, "Yeah, but that is what the chatter is saying."

I say, "Do you have a guess?"

Cleland says, "I have no idea. If it was drugs, the locals would know."

Cass asks him, "Do you know who the business man is?" and he says, "No, I don't. What I do know is everyone seems uneasy when the subject comes up. People are scared, but they don't really know of who."

Cass asks him, "Do you have anything else for me?"

Cleland laughs and says, "Yeah, one more thing, why is Sheriff Branson at Rose's with a woman?"

Cass does not answer Cleland but tells me to get in the SUV. She starts for her door, and Cleland says, "Hey, what about me?"

Cass says, "You don't want to ride back to Rose's with us, do you?"

Cleland says, "No, I guess not, but how about a little something for my trouble?"

Cass says, "Okay, here is a twenty."

Cleland says, "A twenty. That is insulting."

Cass says, "Give me back the twenty, and I will Uber you back to Rose's."

Cleland says, "You are a hard case for a woman."

Cass says, "You mean for a sheriff, don't you?"

Cleland starts to talk, and I hold my hand up and shake my head no. He looks at me, turns, and starts walking.

Cass says, "Didn't I say to get in the car?"

I don't say anything, and I get in the SUV. I get in before Cass as she seems to be gathering herself, and I look back at Dixie and say, "And don't you say anything either."

Dixie looks at me disinterestedly and lays down in the seat. Cass gets in, and I ask, "Where to next, sheriff?"

Cass does a U-turn without talking and heads back toward the Rose's. I think to myself, *Uh-oh*, but I say nothing.

Cass breaks the silence when she asks me, "Did you know they were there?"

I say, "I had no idea, Cass."

When we pull up, I say, "Pull around back please." We do, and there is Buck's truck.

I say, "That's why we didn't see it."

Cass pulls up and parks beside Buck's truck and says, "I am hungry, how about you?"

I say, "Always."

She turns to me and says, "Let's eat."

I say, "You lead, I follow."

She does not take the opening and starts walking toward the door. I say, "You are not going to embarrass me, are you?"

She says, "Probably, yes."

Thank goodness she can't see me grinning as we go inside.

A well-proportioned woman that I assume is Rose walks up and says, "Hello sheriff, are you looking for Buck?"

Cass says, "Good to see you, Rose, and yes, I am looking for Buck."

Rose says, "He is in the back."

Rose asks, "Are you and good-looking there gonna eat?"

Cass says, "Give us a minute and come check please, and he is not that good-looking."

Rose laughs and says, "If you say so, honey."

I smile at Rose, offer my hand, and say, "Good afternoon, ma'am, I am John Young. It is nice to meet you."

Rose offers me her hand, and I take it as she says, "I know who you are. This is a small town, John. Welcome home."

Cass is a little curt as she says, "Can we get moving please?"

I say, "Certainly, sheriff."

Rose gives me a smile and says, "You let me know if there is anything you need, John."

Cass says, "Don't worry, he won't need anything."

I follow Cass as she heads to the backroom quietly. When we walk through the doorway, Joann looks up in surprise, and Buck who had his back to us turns and grins at us sheepishly.

Cass asks them, "What are you guys doing here?"

Joann says, "What does it look like? We are eating supper."

Cass says, "That is not what I meant. Why are you two together?"

Joann says, "Now Cass, I don't need your permission to go on a date."

Buck has not said a word so Cass attacks him next. She says, "My mom doesn't date."

Buck says, "She does now."

Cass starts to say something, and Joann says, "Why don't you and John join us, Cass?"

I interrupt them and say, "Yes, we would love to."

Cass glares at me, but we sit down with them. Rose shows back up and asks what we want to drink and gives us each a menu. As she goes to get our drinks, Joann says, "Cass, I would think that you would be happy for me. You have told me for years I need to date, and now that I am on one, you freak out on me."

Cass says, "I wanted you to date but not Buck."

Joann says, "First of all, it is my decision, but why would you not want me to date Buck?"

Cass says, "Well, because...well, just because I don't want you to."

Joann laughs and says, "It is okay, honey. Buck is a good man, and you need to let him and I go wherever this takes us."

Cass seems to relax a little bit and says to me, "See, I told you everything was going to be fine."

I grin and says, "Why yes, that is exactly what you said."

Joann looks at me knowingly and smiles. Buck just seems relieved that no one is yelling at him, and I am just happy to be here. Rose comes with our drinks and asks us if we are ready to order. I say, "I'm sorry, we have not even looked at the menu yet."

Rose says, "May I suggest the special of the day? It is chicken fried steak with country gravy, mashed redskin potatoes, whole green beans with homemade sweet rolls."

I say, "Sold."

Cass asks her mom what she ordered, and her mom says, "The special."

Cass says, "Mom, you never eat that kind of stuff."

Joann says, "Things change."

Cass says, "What the heck, Rose, bring me the special and some cholesterol medication."

I say to Buck, "What a day, buddy."

Buck smiles that good ole-boy smile of his and says, "Yep." He looks at Joann, smiles, and says, "Things change, don't they, Jo-Jo?"

Cass looks at me and catches me grinning ear to ear, and to my surprise, she smiles at me and says, "If you can't beat 'em, join 'em. Rose, bring me an extra roll and a house salad."

As Rose leaves, I lean back in my chair and listen to the juke box that had been playing since we came in. I close my eyes as Bob Seger sings "Turn the Page." How appropriate. I think I will.

CHAPTER 47

Finding Out Slowly

The food arrives, and it looks and smells fantastic. Rose stands over us as we inspect our food and savor the smell. When she feels we have had the appropriate amount of time to appreciate the presentation, she says, "Okay, who is going to taste their food so I can leave you alone?"

Buck quickly offers to be the test pilot, and Joann laughs and says, "You better hurry. I am hungry."

Buck takes one bite of the steak smiles as he chews, and we all dig in right along with him. Rose watches a moment and says, "Evidently the food is fine," and off she goes.

We don't talk much as we eat, but we all agree that the food is fantastic. As we all start to get our bellies filled, we pick up the conversation again. Buck asks Cass if there are any new developments, and she tells him about the boat search. Buck laughs and says, "I wish I would have been there for that."

I say, "It was fun."

Cass says, "I don't think that *fun* is the right word for it."

I say, "How about interesting, engrossing, fascinating, compelling, or perhaps even captivating?"

Cass says, "Enough already, you are going to mess up my digestion."

Buck says, "Now what about this local business man?"

I say, "Cass and I have talked about that at length, and we just don't know who it might be, unless we are wrong, and it is Sly."

Buck says, "You can bet Sly is involved, but I don't see him being in charge."

Cass says, "That is what we thought too, but we seem to be at a dead end here."

Through this whole conversation, Joann has not spoken, but she has been listening intently. Everyone is sitting quietly being retrospective when Joann says, "Who does Sly hang out with, does he have any friends, where does he go for fun, does he belong to a club?"

Buck says, "You know, I think he belongs to the yacht club down on Creager's Point."

I say, "Can you get us in there, Buck?"

Before he can answer, Joann says, "I can. A membership came with the house. I seldom go there, but I have seen Mr. Braun there."

Cass says, "I forgot you had a membership, Mom, and don't waste the word *mister* on Sly."

Buck says, "Two retired cops, an ex-cop's widow, and a sitting sheriff—what a team."

I say, "It looks like we are fourth and goal, but we don't have a play."

Cass says, "Then we need to go adlib." Cass takes charge and says, "Buck, you and mom go to the yacht club and see what you can find out. John and I are going to do the waterfront scene and kick the bushes.

"Buck, you are paying for supper, I have the tip, and John, you go out and let Dixie out for a little bit while we pay and say our goodbyes to Rose."

I say, "Yes, captain," salute, hug Joann, shake Buck's hand, and head for the SUV.

When I get out to the SUV, I let Dixie out, and I see a guy on a Harley sitting across the road, watching us. I turn and pet Dixie and she takes off to sniff and do her business and when I turn back, the guy is on a cellphone, talking to someone. Cass said to adlib, so I decide to go over and talk to Mr. Biker.

On my way over, he looks up from his call, sees me coming, and starts the bike and takes off. I get a pretty good look at him though, when he turned to look at me as he left. I have a good memory for faces, especially of one that I saw when scanning a bar room for threats. This guy was in the Dive Bar.

Cass comes out the door and sees the Harley leaving and me watching him go and hollers, "What's going on, John?"

I walk over to her and tell her what I know, and she says, "Let's head to the bar."

I say, "Great idea." We load Dixie up and head back up the coast to the Dive Bar. The leads were a trickle at the start, but the faucet is starting to flow a bit more freely. I have done this enough to know that it won't be long before the trickle becomes a gusher.

I look over at Cass and ask her, "Are you okay?"

She says, "Of course I am." I am thinking that I don't really believe her when she asks me the same thing.

I answer just like her and say, "Of course I am."

We both laugh at each other and Cass says, "I think we are going to stop back by the office and put vests on." I tell her I agree that it would be a good idea. I tell her that I have not been shot for a long time and I would like to keep it that way. Cass says, "I have never been shot and I would also like to keep it that way."

I say, "Okay, we are on the same page. We don't want shot today or any day for that matter."

Cass gets us back to the station in remarkable time, and we exit the SUV and quickly enter the station. When we get inside, she tells the deputy at the desk what we need, and he goes after the vests.

While he is gone, another deputy comes in and says he has some information from the blood on the boat. He says, "Sheriff, it is kind of strange, but the blood is from a gang member from New York who has been missing for about six months and was presumed dead. They have his DNA on file from his prison time."

Cass asks the deputy, "How did we get DNA results so quickly?"

The deputy says, "I asked the guy at the lab the same thing," and he said, "He owed Buck a favor."

Cass looks at me and says, "I think Sly is going to need Armani."

CHAPTER 48

Who Wants a Shot?

Cass tells the deputy to put a BOLO out on Sylvester Braun. The deputy says, "Yes, sheriff."

Cass and I put our vests on, check our weapons and ammo supply, look each other over and lock eyes. I break the silence and say, "There is a good chance that this is going to get ugly before it gets over, and there is something I need to say to you."

Cass says, "And I have some things to say to you also, John, but not yet." Cass says, "We know that the guns must still be here somewhere, but where?"

I say, "Let's stick with your plan for the moment and go to the docks and talk to Cindy."

Cass agrees and says, "Let's saddle up, cowboy."

Cass and I go out to the SUV, load up, and head for the Sunset Pier. Once again, we head up the coast and make our way toward a probable showdown. We at least know what kind of people we are dealing with. They are organized and willing to kill.

I tell Cass we might not want to just walk in this time. She agrees, and I tell her I know another way to get in there. She says, "Okay, tell me about it."

I say, "If I remember right, there is a small fishing operation just down the shoreline from the Sunset Pier."

Cass says, "That is right, the Smith boys' dock is kind of hidden from the Sunset Pier." Cass says, "Do you know them?"

I say, "Yeah, we grew up together."

We travel in silence until we get to the turn off for the Smith's place. When we pull up, I see Rick Smith out on the dock handling nets. We get out of the SUV, and this time, we take Dixie with us.

As we approach the dock, Rick sees us and waves. We wave back, and he waves for us to come on out on the dock. Rick is waiting on us and offers his hand saying, "Hi, John, it's been a long time."

I answer, "It sure has, Rick, and you look good."

Rick says, "Then tell my wife. She says I am getting old." Then he turns to Cass and says, "Hello, sheriff, what brings you two out here?"

I ask him, "Do you have a dingy we can borrow for a while?"

Rick says, "Sure do, what you need her for?"

I say, "We need to get up to the Sunset Pier without being noticed."

Rick says, "The water is pretty rough along this area of the coast. How about you just get in my van, and I drive you in? I go in there all the time, no one will even notice me. I will park back behind the Dive shop and go in. You guys can get out the back of the van. No one will even notice you."

Cass says, "Sounds like a good plan, but why you are so willing to help us?"

Rick laughs and says, "Ask John."

Cass looks at me and says, "Did you punch him too?"

I grin and say, "No, I saved his life."

I look over at Rick, and he says, "What are we waiting on?"

As we walk back the dock to his van, Rick asks, "Is that Joseph's dog?"

I say, "Yeah, or at least we think so."

He asks, "How did you end up with her?"

Cass says, "Long story. Let's save it for another day."

Rick says, "Okay then, sounds good." Rick says, "Hop in the back," and I ask him if we can leave Dixie with him. He says, "Sure, no problem."

Cass and I get in back, and Dixie gets in front with Rick. Rick pulls out and makes his way out of the drive and turns toward the

Sunset. Cass looks over at me and says, "So you saved his life. You have led an interesting life, John Young."

I say, "Now that you mention it, I guess I have."

Cass says, "When we get to the pier, you go to the back of the bar, and I will go to the front door."

I say, "If I might suggest that I go in the front, they will not be as stressed as they will be with a uniform in there, and I am not constrained by my position to be as nice as you are."

Cass says, "I don't like it at all, but you are probably right, plus we don't have a warrant."

"If trouble starts, I won't need a warrant."

She gives my hand a squeeze and says, "Don't be stupid, cowboy. And John, you owe me the story of how you saved Rick's life so don't get shot."

I say, "Not today, boss."

The van stops, and we hear Rick get out. We wait a moment and do the same. Cass moves toward the back of the bar, and I head for the front door.

I stand in front long enough to take a breath and clear my thoughts. *Calm mind. Patience, perseverance, and purpose.* I can feel the storm coming, but I am not afraid at all. In fact, I am pumped full of adrenaline, and my senses are heightened. I can hear everything around me, and the smells are all stronger than normal. It will be a bad day for anyone who messes with me today.

I open the front door and the bar goes silent and I see the guy who was on the Harley. I shout out, "Who wants a shot?"

The guy starts to put his hand in his coat as Cass comes through doorway behind the bar gun up and says, "Or better yet, who wants shot?"

She really does "bother me."

CHAPTER 49

Barroom Blitz

I put my hand on my gun and scan the bar, but there is only Harley guy, Cindy, and one other guy in a suit at the bar. Cass tells Harley guy to take his hand out of his coat slowly, and he does, all the while glaring at Cass. I have my eyes on Cindy now, and her hands are still under the bar. I tell her she needs to get her hands where we can see them, but she just looks at me and does not move them.

Cass does not take her eyes off of Harley guy, but says, "Cindy, show John your hands now!"

Cindy says, "They will kill me."

I ask, "Who?"

Cindy's eyes give her away as she glances at the guy in the suit. I look at him, and he still has his back to me. I say, "Mister, you better turn around with your hands where I can see them." He does not answer me, so I say it again only louder. You can feel the tension in the room, and I know that everyone is armed. This could go bad quickly.

Cass stays focused on Harley guy and me on the Cindy and the suit. I say, "Last time I tell you, mister. Hands up and turn."

He does not raise his hands but starts to turn. I say, "Stop and show me your hands."

He makes a quick move to his left, pulls his gun, and shoots Cindy. As she goes down and he turns his gun toward me, I put one in his right shoulder, and he drops the gun. I see Harley guy square up on Cass. She has her hands up open, and I say, "Do you want me to shoot him?" just as her sweep kick buckles him at the knees and the taser hits him in the chest.

I turn to the suit and hear Cass as she calls for the ambulance, and I hear the front door open as two deputies come running in, guns pulled. I tell them to put pressure on the bullet wound in the suit, and I go behind the bar to check on Cindy. Cindy is conscious but bleeding badly.

I put pressure on her wound, and she says, "He came here to make sure I would not talk."

"Who is he?" I ask.

She says, "I don't know his name, but I know who sent him," and she passes out.

By this time, Cass has Harley handcuffed and the ambulance has arrived and they are loading up the unconscious Cindy and the suit. Cass tells the deputies that she wants one of them with the ambulance and the other to follow it to the hospital. She tells them they are to keep a guard on Cindy and the suit and let her know when they wake up—if they wake up.

Another squad car has arrived, and they are loading up Harley to take him to lock up. Cass is sitting at the bar by herself and looking at the mess we have made of the bar.

I walk up and sit down beside her, but I don't say anything, I just sit there by her. I wait patiently for her to speak, and finally she breaks the silence when she says, "That was not fun."

I say, "Is that all you have to say?"

She has a faraway look in her eyes, and I decide to stay quiet. Finally, she says, "Do you get used to this, John?"

I grin at her and say, "Oh yeah, it's second nature to me."

She looks at me a moment and punches me in the arm.

I ask, "What was that for?"

She says, "That one was just on principle."

I say, "What principle is that?"

She quotes Stephen Covey and says, "There are three constants in life: change, choices and principles. I still owe you two punches." I cannot help myself and I laugh out loud. Cass says, "Now answer my question please."

I say, "No, Cass, you don't ever get used to it. People are not supposed to shoot at each other."

She says, "In all the time I have been in law enforcement, that is my first experience with gunfire."

I tell her that she is fortunate, and I remind her that she subdued her assailant without even firing a shot. She smiles at me, and my heart melts again for the first time. This woman is amazing. I can see that something is still on her mind, and I ask her, "What is bothering you, Cass?"

She turns and looks directly in my eyes and says, "The thought flashed through my mind that I might lose you."

I say to her, "It has been a long time since anyone cared whether I was okay, Cass." I am not used to it, but I would like to find out more about that feeling.

Then she gets that playful look in her eyes and says, "Once again, I ask you, have you ever met someone you didn't shoot, punch, or save their life?"

I say, "Yeah, you."

She laughs and puts her hands on mine and says, "I think we have some more work to do, Sheriff Young."

I say, "Retired sheriff, my lady."

Cass grins and says, "My lady. Well, aren't you the gentleman, sir?"

I grin back and say, "Probably not, but you are quite the woman, Sheriff Cass Quince," for which I receive a smile that lights up my world.

Cass and I sit quietly for a moment, and her phone rings. She says, "Just a moment," and puts the phone on speaker. I wait, and I hear Joann's voice. She says, "Buck and I have some information for you."

Cass says, "We will meet you at your house in a half hour, Mom."

I say, "Okay, sheriff, time to gather our wits and make our next move." I say, "Gary Kasparov once said 'I used to attack because it was the only thing I knew. Now I attack because I know it works best.'"

Cass says, "But we are not playing chess, John."

I say, "Yes, we are."

CHAPTER 50

Another Storm

Cass makes a call for the crime scene team to come to the bar, and I say, "Let's go get Dixie from Rick."

When we go outside, Rick is sitting on the porch of the Dive shop, and Dixie is lying beside him. She sees us, jumps up, and runs to us. She goes to Cass first, and I say, "Well, aren't you the fickle, girl?"

Cass rubs her head and says, "We are glad to see you, girl." Dixie gives a woof and turns to me.

I say, "Second fiddle, huh, girl." She gives me a doggy smile, and I say, "Come here, girl."

Rick says, "Well, I don't know what all went on in there, but it sounded like Deadwood."

I laugh and say, "It could have been a lot worse than it was."

Rick says, "I am just glad you two are okay. Let's go get your vehicle." When we get back to Rick's, we say our goodbyes and thank Rick for his help.

I tell him, "We are even now."

Rick says, "I didn't help you to be even, John. I can never pay you back for saving my life. I am eternally grateful."

I say, "Rick, you are a good man, and I know that you have taken the life that God gave you back and used it to help many people. I was in the right place when he needed me to help you. You owe me nothing, Rick. Live your life to the fullest. I hope our paths cross again, but if they don't, 'fare thee well, my friend.'"

Rick tells me goodbye, shakes my hand, and starts to walk away but turns and says, "Thank you, John."

Cass and I leave the dock. She says, "Tell me what happened, John."

I say, "It was nothing."

She says, "John, please tell me the story."

I close my eyes a moment, and I go back to the day of the storm. Rick and I were out pulling crab cages, and we knew a storm was coming, but we wanted to get them all in before it got to us and we lost them.

Rick was manning the lines, and I was steering the boat when the storm cut loose. It hit us with a fury like I had never seen before. I told Rick to forget about the cages and take the loss. We needed to try and get to land. But Rick kept pulling cages.

I was trying to hold the boat into the storm when I turned back to tell Rick we were leaving the cages and heading in. When I turned, it was just in time to see him go over the edge with his leg tangled in the cage line. I tied the wheel and ran back and tried to pull him in, but I couldn't, so I tied myself off and dove in.

I followed the line to him where I cut him free and pulled him out of the ocean. When I got him on the boat, he was not breathing. I did CPR on him, and by God's grace, he came back.

When we got to the shore, I beached the boat and I got him to the hospital. After a couple of days, he got out of the hospital, and from that day, he has lived his life to the fullest. He went from a self-centered, prideful, arrogant young man to a kind thankful and humble man. Our lives went different ways, but obviously he is still thankful. End of story.

Cass says, "Thank you for sharing, John. You act as though all of these events in your life are no big deal. Why is that?"

I say, "Because they aren't."

Cass says, "Oh, but John, they really are. They are what has formed you into the man that I am getting to know. You once said to me that 'life is a lesson.' You and I are learning one right now, and it never stops. I trust you, John, and I like you. This mess we are part of now is just that—a lesson. We get to decide what we take from it by how well we listen. Are you listening, John?"

I am quiet for a moment, and I say, "Yes, Cass, I am listening,"

"Okay, cowboy, let's go see Mom and Buck," she says.

I say, "Let's ride." We load Dixie up and head for the bungalow on the beach.

When we arrive, Buck and Joann are on the porch, drinking iced tea. As we pull up, Dixie gets more and more exited. I say, "Take it easy, girl" as I get out and open the door for her. She is out in a flash and up on the porch.

When Cass and I get up to the porch, Dixie is getting plenty of loving from Joann and Buck. We take a seat on the deck chairs, and Joann asks if we want iced tea. We both say yes, and Joann goes into the house to get it for us.

Buck says, "I hear I missed all the excitement today."

Cass says, "It was nothing."

Buck looks at me and says, "Did you tell her to say that?"

I give Buck a grin and say, "it is all part of the lesson."

Buck asks, "What does that mean?"

I say, "nothing."

Buck says, "Everwhat."

Cass says, "Really?" and I just shrug my shoulders.

Lucky for me, Joann returns with the tea. She gives us each a glass and sits down on the swing with Buck. Buck starts with "We don't have much to tell you. We know that Sly spends time at the club with Mark Hampton." Buck asks me, "Do you remember him, John?"

I say, "Of course, and I saw him on the beach at the crime scene. He is the coroner."

Cass says, "So is that the only person he hangs out there with?"

Buck says, "Mark and some fancy attorney from New York."

Cass and I look at each other and know it must be Armani. The plot is thickening like gravy and corn starch. We all sit in silence, and even Dixie seems restrained. The sun is setting on a long day, but the night is just beginning.

Cass's phone rings again, and it is the deputy at the hospital. Cindy is awake. Cass asks Joann, "Can Dixie stay with you?"

Joann says, "Of course she can."

Buck stands up when we do and says, "Can I help?"

Cass says, "Yes, keep an eye on Mom. These are bad people. Do you have your gun with you, Buck?"

Buck says, "In my truck."

Cass says, "Get it and stay here please."

Buck says, "You got it. Call me if you need me."

We go out and get in the SUV and head for the hospital. It is a quiet trip to the hospital, and when we pull in, Cass says, "Let me do the questioning, John."

I say, "Yes, sheriff, I will follow your lead."

She says, "Thank you, John, and let's go talk to Cindy."

When we get inside, the nurse says, "We have a last name on your perp. It is Leu. Cindy Leu is her full name. No middle name or initial."

I look at Cass, and she grins back at me as I say, "Now we know who Cindy is. She is Cindy Leu, who was no more than two feet away from the guy who shot her."

Cass says, "That is not funny, John."

I say, "Yeah, it is."

She says, "Okay, kind of."

I say when we go in, "I am going to say, 'We are here, we are here, we are here.'"

Cass says, "Listen here, Horton, this is serious business. Unless her doctor's name is Seuss."

We both start laughing, but we settle ourselves before entering the room. Cindy is awake and handcuffed to the bed. She sees us and says, "I am not talking."

Cass asks the deputy if she has been read her rights yet, and he says no one has spoken to her but the doctor and the nurses. Cass reads Cindy her rights, and before she can speak, Cass says, "Before you lawyer up, you have one minute to make a deal. You are welcome to ask for an attorney, but the deal-making is off of the table. Before you answer, remember that you were expendable before, and you still are."

Cindy says, "Give me a moment to think please."

Cass and I step out and wait. A minute later, Cindy yells, "Come back, I am ready to talk."

We walk in together tell the deputy to step outside and close the door. Cindy take a deep breath and says, "This is what I know."

Cass gets out her notebook, and we both take a seat. Cass says, "Start talking."

CHAPTER 51

Cindy Who?

She starts out with "About four years ago, the guy who owned the Dive Shop and Bar wanted to sell both places."

I knew him quite well because I did underwater salvage and wreck diving. He was in a hurry to sell and was asking a fair price, but when I went to the bank, I just could not swing the loan.

Somehow Mr. Braun found out I wanted to buy the place, and he came to see me. He said he would front me the money, but I would have to help him with some import-export work he was going to be involved in. I said that I was not interested in doing anything illegal, and he said that my part of it would be separate of the dirty work. He also said that he needed to run money through my books to launder it. My take would be 20 percent of the money he ran though my books. He has been running about $25,000 a month through the Dive shop and another $10,000 though the bar. You do the math.

Of course, he took most of it for about six months until he had all of the money he loaned me. From that point on, I didn't need any customers, I just kept hiding, making money without much work. All I had to do was to get his boat ready for him when he traveled up the coast to New York and clean it up when he got back.

He was normally gone about seven days each time. Each time before he left, a big white van would come and load crates into the boat and when he got back, the same van would come back and they would unload these large canvas bags like the military would use.

Mr. Braun told me I was to clean up and sanitize the boat immediately upon his return, so as soon as they all left, I would go on board and clean the boat up.

Cass asks, "Did you ever see any evidence of drugs or drug use?"

Cindy says, "No, Mr. Braun hated drugs."

Cass asks her, "What else do you remember, Cindy? You have not helped us much yet."

Cindy thinks a moment, and she says, "You know it was odd, but the same every time, the hold had a weird smell. It was a dry but citrus kind of smell. It was strong but not a bad smell, just strong."

I look at Cass, and I say, "Lime maybe."

Cass asks her, "Did you ever clean up any white powdery substance?"

Cindy said, "Yeah, sometimes there would be traces of white stuff, but it was not dope. It did burn though, if you got it wet."

I say, "Lime."

Cass says to Cindy, "Give us a moment please." We step out of the room, and Cass says, "What the heck would they be transporting that has lime in or with it?"

I think for a bit, and I say, "It makes no sense to me, but the only thing that I know that lime is used for is killing parasites and garden work."

Cass says, "There is another use."

I say, "I know. It is used to cover the smell of a rotting body." I say, "If that is the case, why would Sly have a body in his boat? Sly is no killer."

We go back into the room, and Cindy is just sitting there, staring straight ahead. Cass asks her, "Are you okay, Cindy?"

Cindy says, "No, I am scared."

Cass says, "You should be. You are in a mess here, Cindy. Is there anything else you can think of that might help us?"

She says, "I can't think."

Cass says, "Take a breath and try to relax." Cass says, "We know that Joseph went with him to New York and that sometimes someone else went too. Did you ever see the other guy?"

Cindy says, "I only got a glimpse of him once."

Cass says, "What do you remember about him?"

"It was always dark when they came to board the boat, and one night, I was late getting the boat ready because he did not tell me there would be three of them until later than normal. I had just finished up and I dropped my flashlight and it rolled under the loading ramp. I was under there, getting it, and they pulled up.

"I knew that I was not supposed to see the third guy, so I just stayed under the ramp. When they walked up the ramp, all I could see was that he was taller than Mr. Braun and they were talking and laughing, and I heard Mr. Braun call him Bones. I think it was a nickname because the guy said, 'Don't call me that.'"

Cass asks her, "Is that all you remember?" and she says, "Yes."

Cass says, "Okay, Cindy, we are leaving a guard here. They already tried to kill you once. We will protect you."

Cindy hollers at us as we walk out, "Hey, what are you going to do with me?"

Cass says, "Keep you alive."

We make our way over to the suits' room. He is also handcuffed to his bed by arm and leg. He is also still unconscious from surgery. We talk to the guard and the nurse and tell them we need to talk to him as soon as he wakes up. The nurse says he lost a lot of blood, and he is in critical condition.

Cass says, "Let's go back to the station and process what we know."

As we walk out to the SUV, Armani pulls up. We stop and wait on him to get out of his car. He sees us and walks over to us. He says, "I am here to talk to my clients."

Cass asks him, "What clients do you mean?"

He says, "The two you have in the hospital."

Cass says, "One of them declined counsel, and the other one is unconscious and has not been identified yet. Can you identify him for us?"

Armani says, "I will wait until he wakes up to make sure who it is." Then he turns and goes back to his car.

I say to Cass, "That guy is a piece of high-dollar crap."

Cass laughs and says, "Yeah, but he is still crap."

I say, "No arguments here."

We get in the SUV and head back to the station. We make the drive silently, both of us processing the events of the day.

CHAPTER 52

Sunshine and Rainbows

When we are back in Cass's office, we both sit down, and the weight of the day's events settles on us. I look at Cass and say, "I think I might be wearing down."

Cass says, "Thank heavens you said it first. I am exhausted."

We talk for a little while about the clues we have so far, but we realize that we are just too tired to make heads or tails of them. Cass says, "We have to get some sleep, John," and I agree with her.

I say, "I will head back to the motel," and before I can finish, Cass says, "No, you won't, you are coming home with me. I have an extra bedroom, and you are going to stay there tonight."

I can't think of any solid reason to say no. It is late, and I am also exhausted. Cass does not wait for a response and says, "All right then, it is decided. Let's go."

I say, "A good night's sleep may give us a new perspective."

We leave the station, and Cass calls her mom and asks her if she will keep Dixie tonight, and she says of course. She tells Cass that they went and got Buck some fresh clothes, and he is going to sleep on the couch tonight at her house. Cass is silent for a moment and says, "Good idea, Mom."

I have been listening to the conversation, and I decide it would be best to stay quiet. I have a feeling that Cass would agree with me.

We make the drive to her house in relative silence, and when we pull up, I see a very quaint little one-story home with a nice front porch and a one-car garage. I can tell there is a creek beside the house, but I can't see it very well.

Cass parks in front of the garage and says, "Come on, cowboy, let's get some sleep."

I get my duffle out of the back of the SUV as Cass goes up to the side door by the garage and puts in the key code and opens the door. When we walk in, and she turns on the light, I see a completely different side to the sheriff. The kitchen is perfect. I say, "I would love to cook in this kitchen."

Cass says, "It is my favorite place in the whole house. I sit here in the mornings and watch the sun come up over the creek and the mist on the water is almost surreal sometimes." Cass says, "It may be simple, but it is mine."

I ask her, "May I have the tour, madam?"

She says, "But of course, good sir." Cass shows me the house, which does not take long because it is only about 1700 square feet, but it is wonderful. I think about my house in Raleigh, and I am embarrassed about the size of it. I realize that I only live in just a small part of the overall house.

Then I realize that I am thinking of and calling the place I live a house, not my home. I wonder, *When was the last time I was home?*

I come to the startling conclusion. The answer is now.

I come up out of my thoughts to find Cass watching me. She asks me, "Are you back?"

I ask, "What did you say?"

She says, "I asked you if you were back, back from whatever you were thinking about."

I grin and say, "Yes, sorry, my mind was off somewhere else."

She says, "Yes, John, I know. Welcome back. Let me show you to your room." I follow Cass down the hall to my room. She opens the door and says, "You have your own bathroom, the fridge has stuff to eat or drink, and you are welcome to anything you need or want."

I say, "Thank you, Cass, this has been quite a day. You are a special woman and a great sheriff."

Cass says, "You ain't so bad yourself, cowboy."

I smile and say, "Goodnight, Cass."

She says, "Sleep well, John, and set your alarm for 5:00a.m. Breakfast at 6:00a.m., and you are cooking. Oh yeah, Buck and Mom will be here too. Goodnight." And before I can ask what I am supposed to make for breakfast, she was gone.

I have to laugh. I am not used to being told what to do, and it does not seem to bother me at all. What a crazy two days it has been.

I get undressed and I say a little prayer and the pillow is soft and the bed is warm and I am wide awake for about one minute. Sometime in the night, I dream of a time down at the beach when I was about twelve years old.

Me, Ron, and Joseph are playing in the rocks up on the ledge overlooking the ocean when Joseph hollers for us to come over to where he is. Ron and I run over there, and Joseph is looking into a crevice in the rocks. He says, "It is a caveman's cave."

Ron and I laugh at him, and Ron says, "There are no cave men here."

Joseph gets mad at us and says, "I don't mean now, I mean it was." Joseph says, "Let's go in there and check it out."

I wake up to the sound of my alarm on my phone going off and see it is 5:00a.m. already. I get clean clothes out of my duffle and go into the bathroom and turn on the shower. As I get undressed, I think about the dream and then it comes to me.

When I finish my quick shower and towel dry my hair, I get dressed and go out to the kitchen. First things first, I find the coffee pot, and of course, everything I need is in the cupboard above it. Nice.

I open the fridge and search the contents. I see eggs, ham, shredded cheese, a small onion, and a bell pepper and some fresh mushrooms. There are a few potatoes in there, also a tube of bake, and serve biscuits. Amazing, it could have been my fridge I was looking in.

I look through the drawers and cupboards and find all the pans I need, and I start cooking. When Cass comes in the kitchen, the coffee is ready, and the food is getting close. She says, "John, it smells wonderful in here. I have never had a man cook for me here, ever."

I smile and say, "It is an honor, my lady." I say, "We have a little bit before everything is ready so let's have a cup of coffee and look out the window."

Cass laughs that Christmas bell laugh, and I pour us two cups of coffee. We are just starting to settle in when I hear the door open, and in come Joann, Buck, and Dixie.

Once again, Dixie goes to Cass first. I look at her and say, "Hey, did you forget who saved you?"

Dixie tilts her head and looks at me and woofs as if to ask, "Who saved who?"

Buck laughs at me and says, "Good morning, John. Good morning Cass."

Joann comes in over and hugs Cass then me and heads for the coffee pot and pours two more cups. Buck and Joann take a seat at the table with us, and out of nowhere, we all start laughing.

Joann breaks the moment by saying, "Look at us, we were all living our lives like we did not need anyone, and here we are."

Before it can get to serious, I say, "Breakfast is ready to serve."

Cass and her mom get up and get table settings ready, and Buck helps me get the food on. We have a nice Frittata, fried potatoes with onions and peppers and biscuits. This time, Joann asks Buck to ask the blessing and he does not flinch as he asks us to take hands and he gives a simple heartfelt prayer.

When he ended the prayer, I see Joann give his hand an extra squeeze as we release. It makes me smile, and Buck sees me looking and says, "Mind you own business, buddy."

I grin and say, "She is my business."

Cass says, "Easy, boys. Let's eat."

Buck and I grin at each other as we wait on the ladies to fill their plates. Who could have known this was going to happen? Not me or Buck, that's for sure.

Breakfast is filled with laughter and fun-loving pokes and good stories, and when we are done, we clean up the kitchen together. It feels like a family dinner. It has been a long, long time. If home is where the heart is, I am home.

Once again Cass catches me off in space. She splashes me with dish water and says, "Welcome back," when my thought ends, and I return to the dishwater.

I say, "Hey. You could get soap in my eyes."

She says, "Big baby."

I say, "Maybe." When I look over at Joann and Buck, they are in their own little world. This is too cute.

"What is wrong with me?" Cass says. "Okay, people, back to reality now. Let's talk.

CHAPTER 53

It's Dark in Here

Cass has us all take a seat, and we position ourselves without instruction. Cass at the head of the table, me at the other end, and Buck and Joann across from each other. Cass takes charge as she goes over the limited information we have at this point. When she is through, Buck goes over the list of potential "Bones" in town.

As he brings each one up, there just does not seem to be anyone who fits the bill. When he has exhausted the list of possibilities, I tell them about my dream. Cass asks, "Does the cave actually exist?"

I answer her, "Yes, it does. The three of us went back the next day with flashlights to explore it. We didn't tell anyone because Grandma would not have let us go. If you are looking up at the ledges from below, you would have no idea that there is a cave up there. I don't think anyone in my family knew it was there, and if they did, they never told us because they knew we would not stay out of it.

"It was not hard to get to if you knew how. The flat area that ran down to it from the top was also hidden behind an outcropping. It was a cool place for us to play and hide, but we grew out of it quickly. It was deadly dark, but it was dry, and good-sized."

I told them I had not thought about it for years and years. "One time when we were playing there, we went in with only one flashlight and Joseph dropped it and it went out. We were not in too far, so we were able to crawl out. It scared us so badly, we never went back in. I think we should to go back to the plantation and check out that cave. It would be a great place to hide guns or a person."

Cass says to me, "You better take off those cowboy boots and put back on those patrol boots, Marshall Dillon."

I agree, and Buck says, "When you crawl into a foxhole, the fox has the advantage."

Joann, who has been listening this whole time, now chimes in with "Cass, you need to be careful out there."

Cass says, "Mom, please try to remember I am the sheriff. This is my job."

Joann says, "Don't you worry, I never forget."

I say, "I hate to interrupt this family reunion, but we need get moving."

Cass agrees with me, and we both get up from our chairs to leave. We go through the handshaking and hugging again, and Cass says, "I forgot to feed Dixie."

Joann says, "But I didn't."

I tell her, "Thank you," and Buck says, "What do you want me to do?"

Cass says, "With all this bad element in town, I think you should stay with Mom."

Buck says, "Okay, but I could help you."

Cass says, "I know you could, Buck, but you taught me everything I know, and I am ready for this."

Buck says, "Remember, you two, calm mind."

I say, "Thank you, Buck. I never forget what you taught me."

Cass says, "What do you think about taking Dixie with us?"

"I think we should," I say. She is a built-in alarm system. Cass asks her mom to lock up when she leaves, and the three of us go out to the SUV. Cass open the trunk and checks out the flashlights for our spelunking trip while I let Dixie out to do her business. Everything checks out, and Dixie is done so once again we load up to head for the plantation. T here is an air of tension hanging over us, and I need to break it, so I ask Cass, "Which one hangs from the ceiling and which one points up, stalactite or stalagmite?"

Cass says, "Do I look like a geologist to you?"

I say, "Now that you mention it, I think you do. A sheriff geologist. You could be in charge of law enforcement at the Hard Rock Café."

Cass is grinning, and I am feeling pretty good about my joke-telling ability when she says, "Then I guess it's time to rock." She bothers me. I have to laugh at her, and the tension is broken.

Dixie is sitting up in the backseat, and she obviously knows that something is going on. Cass says, "How about some music?" and turns on the radio. The song is "Rock Around the Clock," and we start laughing again. I have to say that the day has started off well, but I am pretty sure it will get worse before it gets better.

When we get to the plantation, I show Cass an old service road that seems to be dry enough that we can use it to get closer to the beach but not so close as to be heard approaching. When we get as far as we can go, we pull over and unload. Dixie is anxious but stays close to us as we get what we need from the back of the SUV and put our vests on again.

Once we are geared up, Cass says, "This time you lead, John." I take the lead, and we start the trek for the beach. We move quietly and cautiously with Dixie in front sweeping back and forth, nose to the ground. When we come into sight of the cliffs, I tell Cass to stay close to me and right behind me.

We make our way up the graded area and start to work our way up into the rocks. The spot I am looking for comes into view now, and I point to it for Cass. We pull our weapons at the same time, and there is no sound but the waves on the beach and the gulls. We are in stealth mode now, and I can see the outcropping that protects the entrance to the cave.

Dixie is at my feet now and I can hear her growling softly and the muscles in her body are strung tight. I can tell by her reaction to this place that Joseph is here.

I hold my hand out, and Cass hands me the stun grenade. I get as close to the entrance as I can, and I pull the pin and step around the outcrop and throw the grenade in.

As it explodes, a series of gunshots come screaming out of the cave and rock explodes all around me and I feel an impact on my cheek as I dive back for cover. The shooting stops, and I wave for Cass to move in with me.

Joseph is right inside the entrance, blinded and holding his ears from the impact of the stun grenade. He is disabled, and his gun is lying beside him. I kick it away, and Cass pushes him down with her knee in his back and handcuffs him. She looks up at me and says, "You are bleeding, John."

I wipe my hand over my cheek, and it comes away bloody. I grab my hanky and wipe my face off then I sweep the flashlight over the inside of the cave, and I see the crates of guns along the wall. Dixie is still outside the entrance and seems to have no interest in coming in. I tell her to guard the entrance, and she sits right in front of it.

Cass has Joseph sitting up now, and he still can't hear but his head is clearing. He is looking at me, and he says way too loud, "I should have known you would remember."

I don't say anything to him and walk over to look at the guns. The first 9mm I pick up has the serial number filed off, and each gun I look at after is the same way. Joseph is watching but not talking.

Cass goes outside and calls her team to come in and get the guns and sweep the area. I walk over to Joseph and pull him up and take him outside. I ask him if he can walk, and he nods his head yes. We will have to wait for about an hour for the team to get there, but we can't leave the guns.

Cass waves for me to come over to her, and she tells me that the deputy told her that the judge released Butch Wagner on bail. Great, one more bad guy on the street again.

We both turn back to Joseph when a bullet slams into the rocks by Joseph's head. I grab him, and we all dive back into the cave. Joseph says, "They are here."

CHAPTER 54

Cave Dwellers

I tell Cass, "We are in the same predicament that Joseph was. There is no way out of here."

I look over at Joseph and ask him, "Why did you take the guns?"

He glares at me but does not answer, and I tell him, "They will kill you too, you know."

He says, "Yes, I know."

Cass says, "One of us needs to make sure they can't get to close to us. We need to hold out until the team gets here."

I say, "True, but they are going to walk into an ambush also."

Cass pulls out her phone, but she can't get a signal in the cave. She says, "We can't warn them if I can't get out of this cave."

I kneel over by Joseph and ask him what the heck is going on around here. He says, "Why do you care? You have been gone for years, cousin."

I ask him "What did you call me?"

He says, "I called you cousin."

I say, "I thought you did not believe me."

He says, "I didn't, but when I was going through mom's stuff after she died, I found a letter from your grandma to my mom."

I look at him incredulously and say, "Grandma knew?"

He says, "Yeah, she did. She told my mom in her letter that if she ever told me, she would ruin my family."

I asked Joseph if he knew what happened to Gary. Joseph said no. As far as he knew, he just never came back. I say, "That's the story." That gets Joseph's attention.

But before we can go any further, we hear a gunshot and what sounds like Buck yelling, "Get on your knees!"

We all get quiet, and we hear this: "It is Buck. I am coming in, don't shoot me."

Cass and I look at each other and wait on Buck to get down to us. We move out of the cave opening, and we can see him coming with a guy in handcuffs.

Joseph yells, "Hey, Buck, you're kind of old for this stuff, aren't you?"

I tell Joseph to keep his mouth shut and turn to watch Buck bring his prisoner in. When he gets to us, the first thing Cass says is "Where is my mom?"

Buck laughs and says, "Yes, I am fine, and your mom is at the station. As soon as you guys left the house, I took Joann to the station and followed you out here, but I came in from Joseph's place so no one would see me coming, including you guys."

I say, "I, for one, am pretty happy about it."

Cass says, "Yeah, me too." Cass asks Buck, "What about the shot we heard?"

Buck says, "The shooter was not as fortunate as this guy. He refused to put his gun down, so I put him down." Buck says, "I have never seen the shooter before, but this is the guy that you brought in and that the judge released this morning."

Cass finishes for him. "Butch Wagner."

Buck says, "Yeah, that guy."

Cass asks, "Buck, do you know which judge left him out on bail?"

Buck says, "Sure do, Sly's buddy, Judge Clifton."

Cass is hot, and I don't blame her. The guy he left out just tried to kill us and/or Joseph.

We wait for a little while longer, and Cass has the team on the phone, directing them in to us. She tells them she wants radio silence, cellphones only. When they arrive, we give them Joseph and Butch. Cass says to the deputy, "Don't let anyone know we have prisoners or that John and I are okay. Maintain radio silence, cellphone only until I tell you different. Lock these two up, and don't let them talk to each other."

I love a leader with a plan. Oh, did I say love? I mean, I respect a leader with a plan.

Cass has a fire in her eyes that I have not seen before. Someone is going to not be happy to see her. She tells the team we are taking one of the ATVs they brought to the scene to get back to her vehicle.

I say, "May I please drive this time?" and she grudgingly says, "Yes."

I get on the ATV, and she gets on behind me. I say, "Put your arms around me, sheriff," and she whispers, "Not until we are out of sight."

I laugh and hit the throttle, and she throws her arms around me to stay on. I move out hard and fast so she can't let go of me. I am laughing and enjoying myself way too much for her, and as soon as we slow down, she lets me know about it. She says, "You think you are pretty smart, don't you, cowboy?"

I say, "I don't know about pretty, but I am smart."

She punches me hard in the arm and I look in the side mirror at her and she is smiling. Man, is she pretty. When we get back to the SUV, I realize we forgot Dixie and turn to tell Cass just as Dixie catches up with us. She is panting, but she seems to be just fine. I bend down and pet her and tell her what a good girl she is, and she gives me her doggy grin again.

We leave the keys under the seat of the ATV and load up in her SUV. I don't ask to drive this time. I do, however, ask her where we are going, and she tells me, "Back to the Dive shop."

I say, "I think that is a good idea," and she says, "Of course it is."

She grins and throws stones as she peels out. She turns the lights and siren on this time and says, "Hang on, big boy. My turn."

CHAPTER 55

Everywhere We Look

Cass drives like Richard Petty all the way back to Sunset Pier, and we pull up in front of the Dive shop and get out of the SUV but leave the lights flashing. There is crime scene tape over the door of the Dive Shop and the bar.

We both pull our guns and make our way slowly up to the door of the Dive Shop. The crime scene tape is intact, but there is a window broken out. Cass breaks the tape in front of the door, pulls her gun up, looks at me, and puts three fingers up and counts down. Three, two, one…and kicks the door open.

I go in first, and she is right behind me. We scan the room, and it has been ransacked. We slowly work our way through the store main are and into the back room. It is the same there also. Someone tore it apart. We both say clear from opposite ends of the back room when we hear a vehicle start and tear out of from behind the dive shop.

I run to the front door, and I see an old Ford truck fly out of the parking lot and onto the main road—a truck missing the front bumper.

Cass calls in and puts out an APD on an older Ford truck missing a front bumper and reminds them phones only. She says, "Let's go over and check out the bar again."

When we get there, we find the same thing—window broken, and the place has been flopped just like the Dive Shop. Cass asks me, "What do you think they were looking for?"

I say, "I don't know, but I am guessing money or a ledger of some kind tracking money." I say, "If it was important enough to come back to the crime scene, I would guess it was a ledger or records of some kind."

Cass says, "I think we need to go talk to our prisoners before we make another move."

I agree and we get back in the SUV and this time she turns the lights off and we drive back to the station like normal people in a hurry—a big hurry. On the way, she says, "Let's pop into the hospital and check on Cindy and no-name."

We get there in about ten minutes and go to the nurse's station to check on the status of our prisoners-slash-patients. The nurse at the desk tells us that Cindy is doing well and that no-name is awake but still in serious condition.

When we get to Cindy's room, she is awake and watching the Andy Griffith show. Cass walks up to her bed and turns off the TV. Cindy says, "Hey, I was watching that."

Cass says, "Not anymore." Cass asks Cindy if she has remembered anything else about guy number three, and she says, "Yeah, I remembered one more thing."

Cass asks her, "Well, what is it?"

Cindy says, "After he called him Bones, Mr. Braun said, 'I don't know how you ever get used to this.' He answered, 'It's just part of the job.'"

Cass says, "Is that all?"

Cindy says, "Yes, that is all I remember."

As we walk, Cass tells the nurse to shut Cindy's TV off, and we go to no-name's room. His TV is on also. He is awake but groggy. C

Cass and I step up to his bed as he slurs out the words "So you two are still alive."

Cass says, "Alive, kicking, and mad. I am tired of being shot at, and I want some answers."

No-name laughs and coughs and says, "You won't be getting any from me."

The nurse comes in and says, "He really is in no shape to answer questions right now."

Cass says, "Okay, shut off his TV too."

As we walk out to the SUV, Cass says, "Everywhere we go, someone is lying to us, shooting at us, or won't talk to us. I am getting a complex, John."

We get back in SUV again and finish the drive back to the station. I kind of expect to see the Armani's car there, but it is not. When we get inside, the deputy says, "The prisoners are both in isolation cells." He also tells us that he called the coroner, and Mark came and picked up the body and took it back to the funeral home for the autopsy and that he left with it before they could get prints.

Cass says, "Okay, we will go over to the funeral home when we are done talking to the prisoners."

Cass tells the deputy bring Joseph to the interrogation room, and we go in to wait on him. Cass says, "I think that having you in here will rattle him, John."

I say, "I am not sure but okay."

When Joseph comes in, he has an arrogant look on his face, and he does not seem at all worried about his situation. He is cuffed, and Cass tells him to take a seat across from us. He does so and says, "I am a dead man."

Cass asks him, "What does that mean?"

He says, "Wherever I go, they will have me killed."

Cass asks him, "Who will have you killed?"

He says, "The Irish mob."

I ask him, "Is that who the guns were for?"

He says, "Yes."

Cass tells him, "If there is any chance at all we can help you, it will take you telling us everything you know, Joseph."

Joseph says, "Unless you can put me in a witness protection program, it does not matter what I say or don't say. I am still a dead man walking." He says, "Unless you can guarantee that in writing, I can't help you."

Cass says, "It would take the Feds to guarantee that, Joseph."

He says, "Call them."

Cass says, "I will call them if you give me the name of the big boss on this end and what is being shipped back here. I want the man in charge in my county. The Feds will want the Irish Mob."

Joseph says, "The only thing I will tell you is what is in the bags."

Cass feigns not knowing about the bags and says, "What bags?"

Joseph says, "The bags with the bodies in them."

Cass and I look at each other in disgust but knowing it is true. I say, "Before you lawyer up, Joseph, who knocked me on the head?"

Joseph says, "That was the guy you found on the beach. I shot him. I told them that you were coming home, and we should not do the last shipment until after you left again, but they got greedy and tried to squeeze in one more.

"We had a man watching you in Raleigh, and when you left earlier than we planned, I went to the plantation and moved the guns. They were going to kill you, but when the guns were gone, there was no point in it. Still, you caught one of them on your place when you got there, and he cold-cocked you so he could get away.

"I was watching from my ATV out in the woods, and when he tried to get away, he ran right to me. He had parked his old Ford truck at my place and hiked over to yours. We argued, and he pulled a knife on me and I shot him and hauled him to the beach where my partner took him up the coast and dumped him."

I say, "Any chance you will tell us who your partner was?"

To my surprise, he says, "Sure, it was Sly."

I look over at Cass and ask, "Is the BOLO still out on Sly?"

She says, "Yes, it is."

I say to Joseph, "One more thing. Was it you that warned me to leave?"

Joseph says, "Yes."

I ask him, "Why?"

He says, "Because you are family." I don't know what to say to that, and Joseph says, "Get me my lawyer now."

Cass and I get up and go out to her office to talk. We walk in and she takes her seat behind the desk and I take one across from her. We sit there in silence for quite a while. Finally, she asks me, "Are you okay, John?"

I say, "Yes, I am."

She says, "Then we have some more work to do."

I say, "Yes, we do."

She says, "Are you thinking what I'm thinking?" and I say, "Yes, I believe I am. Let's go get him."

CHAPTER 56

Dead Pool

We get back out to the SUV, and we check our vests, weapons, and ammo and decide we are good to go. This time we go silent, and we park around the corner from the Hampton Funeral Home and Crematorium.

We get out of the SUV and make our way around the back of the funeral home. When we get back behind where they unload the bodies, we see Sly's black Navigator parked up in the loading bay. We move along the tree line until we come to a storage building behind the main building.

I look in the window, and I can see pile of tarp material bags with white powder all around them. I motion for Cass to look in, she does, and we nod to each other. We were right.

We now work our way up along the side of the main building. As we near the loading dock, we can hear two men's voices, and they are arguing. We can tell one of them is Sly, but I don't recognize the other voice, and I can't see him.

I whisper to Cass, "Is it him?" and she nods "yes."

We are just about to announce ourselves when I hear a twig break behind us. I yell, "Get down!" just as the slug hits the wall above our heads.

From my prone position, I look for the shooter, and I see him duck behind a tree. I squeeze off a round to let him know I saw him, and it slams into the tree he is behind. I motion for Cass to continue up to the loading dock, and I pop off three shots to keep our shooter at bay while she moves up by the dock. My Glock has the large-capacity magazine and holds fifteen rounds, and I rattle off a few more toward our adversary's position.

Behind me, I hear shots ring out and not from Cass's gun. I hear her yell, "You are not getting out of here!" And then I hear her fire off a few rounds.

In the meantime, my guy is pinned down behind that tree, and he has to get in the open to move. I think for a moment and decide to try something. I dig around, and I find a pinecone. I pick it up, and I yell, "He is to your right!" and I throw the pinecone to my left as far as I can. It hits the ground, and my guy steps out from the tree and fires. My shot catches him in the back, and down he goes.

I move over and check him for a pulse. He is dead.

As I move up to help Cass, I think, *Wait until I tell Buck about that move.*

When I reach Cass, she says, "They are behind the van and can't get to the door without coming out in the open."

I say, "Let's try and talk them out."

Cass yells at them, "This will end badly for both of you if you don't surrender right now!" They respond with gunfire, and Cass yells, "So is that a no?"

I fire a couple of rounds back at them to remind them we are not giving up either. Cass says, "Okay, one last chance. If one of you will testify against everyone else, I will cut you a deal."

I hear them arguing, and I can hear Sly saying, "I don't plan on dying here tonight. I will take my chances with the law." He hollers, "Don't shoot! I am coming out." He walks out from behind the van with his hands up. He takes about four steps, and I hear the shot and see the look of surprise on his face as he topples forward.

Cass says, "I trusted you, Mark."

Mark yells back, "I died years ago when my mother died! You can't hurt me, sheriff."

I say, "Mark, this does not have to end this way. We can get you help."

Mark says, "Of all people, John, you know what we talked about that day at the creek. I let my mother's death define me. I chose to die with her. From that day forward, it did not matter what I did. My life was over anyway.

"When Sly said he had someone who wanted to talk to me from New York, and that could make a lot of money with him, I said sure. They needed a place to get rid of dead bodies, and I had a crematory. It was a match made in hell. I said why not? Sly was already shipping guns up there so all he had to do was bring bodies back for me to dispose of, and then you came home. Sly and Joseph tried to protect you instead of just letting us kill you. Now look at the mess they have caused. Sly is dead, and I don't know where Joseph is.

Cass yells back "Joseph is in my jail, and he is talking!"

Mark says, "It does not matter, we are all dead men anyway."

Cass says, "If you surrender right now and help us, maybe we can keep you off of death row Mark."

Mark says, "Why would I want to do that?" It gets very quiet as Cass and I wait for Mark to respond. When he responds, it is not the answer we were hoping for. It is a single gunshot and a thud as his body hits the floor.

Cass and I move carefully up to the van until we see the blood on the floor by the tire. We holster our guns and walk around the van to find Mark bleeding from a gunshot wound to the head. Cass checks him for a pulse, and he does not have one.

Cass plops down on the floor beside Mark's body and says, "I worked with him for years, and I had no idea."

I say, "Cass, this is not your fault."

She says, "Yes, I know that, John, and I might feel different if I did not know the story of his mom and your dad. The lesson never ends does it, John?"

I say, "No, it doesn't."

By the time Buck and the other deputies start arriving, Cass has gathered herself and is back in charge of the situation. She tells Buck to call the coroner from the county next to ours and to call the state patrol for support also. The state troopers get there quickly, and the EMS people are also quick to respond.

While all of this is going on, I see a black sedan pull up. I think, *Feds*, and I was right. Two men both in expensive black suits get out of the car and walk up to Cass. One of them asks her, "Are you Sheriff Quince?"

She says, "Yes, I am. How can I help you gentleman?"

The shorter one of the two says, "Ma'am, we are with the FBI. My name is agent Maxwell, and this is agent Donovan. We will be taking over this scene and investigation."

Cass starts to protest, and I say, "Don't do it. You are better off this way."

She looks at me and says, "You are probably correct, retired Sheriff John Young. Let's let these men do their jobs."

As we walk away, agent Donovan says, "We will need your paperwork and statements from all of you."

Cass says, "Not until tomorrow you won't," and we keep walking.

Buck falls in behind us, and we go find Cass's SUV and head for the station. When we get back to the station, we go into Cass's office and fall into our chairs.

I say, "It is barely past noon, and I am exhausted."

We sit in silence for a little while letting the events of the day wash over us when I realize my brother and his family will be at the airport today at 4:00p.m. I tell Cass and Buck this, and they say, "Let us help you, John."

CHAPTER 57

My Old Front Porch

Cass takes me, Dixie, and my duffel bag back to her house so I can take a shower and put on fresh clothes. We don't talk much as we make the short trip. Even Dixie is subdued.

We arrive at her house, and when I walk in, I think to myself, *I have more good memories with Cass in the last three days then I have made in the last ten years.*

I am sitting on the bed with Dixie at my feet when I hear a tap on the door and Cass walks in. She surprises me and sits down beside me. She claps her hands together and lays them on her lap and asks me what I am thinking. I don't know if I should tell her, but she says, "It is okay, John, just say it."

I take a breath and tell her what I just thought about. She takes my hands in hers and says, "Look at me, John." I turn my gaze to her beautiful eyes. They have a smile in them that makes my heart jump in my chest. She asks me, "Are you still going to sell the plantation, John?"

I say, "Why do you ask that?"

She says, "Because I think it is so much a part of you that selling it would be like selling a part off of your body."

I laugh and say, "Maybe I could trade it for a new nose. This one is kind of big."

Cass gives me a playful punch in the shoulder and says, "Could you be serious for a minute please?"

I grin and say, "Sorry, it is my way of deflecting emotions."

Cass says, "I know, John, you have been doing it for three days."

I say, "Ouch."

Cass says, "Listen to me, cowboy, I am only going to say this one time. I want you to stay here. We need to find out what this thing we have is, and if it is meant to last." She gets up and says, "There is a towel in the cupboard in the bathroom. You need to get ready," and she leaves the room.

Dixie looks up at me like, "What just happened here?"

I rub her head and say, "I think I am falling in love, girl." Dixie gives me her doggy grin, a soft woof, and lays her head back down.

When I am done in the shower and dressed, I go out to the kitchen, and Cass is already there waiting on me. She laughs and says, "Will I always be waiting on you to get ready?"

I say, "I hope so."

We both laugh and head for the SUV. Cass goes through a car-wash on the way back to the plantation as her SUV was a mess after the last three days. I say, "You didn't need to wash it for my family."

She grins and says, "You only get to make one first impression."

I agree that is true. and I think about the first impression I got when she showed up at the plantation. I am sitting there in my seat grinning, and Cass says, "Why are you grinning, cowboy?"

I say, "I met a girl."

She says, "I feel sorry for her."

I say, "You should."

We both laugh, and the trip to the plantation seems to take only a moment. I see the old gate coming up on the right and Cass turns on her turn signal and turns into the drive back to the plantation and we slowly make our way back to the old house. I see my truck is still in the same spot as Cass pulls up and stops the SUV. She puts it in park, and we sit quietly in our respective seats.

Cass breaks the silence and says, "Buck and I are going to meet your family at the airport, John. We will greet them and make sure they get their rentals, help them load up and lead them back here. Unless you would rather meet them alone."

I look in her eyes and say, "Please come back with them and bring Buck and Joann with you."

Cass says, "May I walk with you back to the place this all started, John?"

I say, "I would be honored if you were to accompany me, my lady."

I get my duffel and my Dixie out of the SUV, and we walk up the steps onto the porch together. I lay my stuff down and turn to Cass. She does not flinch as she looks deeply into my eyes. I think to myself, *Should I kiss her?* and she leans into me and offers her lips up to mine and we kiss softly.

I hold her in my arms and I say, "Thank you, Cass."

She smiles at me and says, "This is gonna be fun."

I respond, "I love it when you say that."

She steps out of my arms and says, "Get yourself ready for your family, John." She turns and walks back to her SUV, starts it up, waves at me, and leaves.

I stand there for a little while and look around me, smiling. I take my seat on the porch swing cautiously, but it holds me. I lean back into the memories, and Dixie takes her place at my feet. I tell God that I am grateful for my life, for the trials, and for the hardships and for the victories.

I smile a thankful smile, and I know "he" sees. I wipe away a tear of joy, and I know "he" cares. I say I am thankful, and I know "he" hears. I sit quietly and listen as the plantation comes to life. I also have come back to life.

In my mind, I hear, "Patience, perseverance, purpose. The Lesson is not over, John."

To be continued.

ABOUT THE AUTHOR

Randy resides in Auburn, Indiana and is the father of three children and five grandchildren. He is a man of faith and has seen many challenges in his life. Randy knows firsthand the power of God's forgiveness and restoration. This novel is a pilgrimage into those topics combined with a fictional mystery. Please join him as he takes us on one man's journey into redemption.

CPSIA information can be obtained
at www.ICGtesting.com
Printed in the USA
FFHW021703110819
54212636-59941FF